CURSED WOLF

HOWLING DEATH MC
BOOK THREE

SOPHIE ASH

CONTENT WARNING

This book contains the following:

- Car accident (collision with an animal, no explicit gore and the animal lives)
- Sexual harassment by a work superior
- Explicit sex
- Dirty talk
- Biting (mating bites)

CHAPTER I

EMMALINE

I was in no shape to drive home in the state I was in. Tears blurred my vision as I sat in my silent, motionless car, and my chest felt like it was going to cave in on itself.

The veterinary clinic had just closed and darkness blanketed the winding mountain road ahead. No street lights could be found out here. Those were only dotted sparsely throughout Fulsburg's single, tiny residential neighborhood and the downtown strip that covered all of two blocks. The rest of this remote mountain town only had their cars' headlights and the starry sky to see at night.

When I first moved here, I found it eerie how dark it could really get without lights from a city. How quiet it could be when you lived near the mountains in a population of under a thousand and your neighbors were retirees that went to bed by eight pm.

It was a clear night and the stars were out in full force, along with the moon in a bright silver crescent. The stars and moon felt like an audience, even though I was finally alone in my car.

I swiped angrily at my tears to clear my vision, but my eyes just welled up again. The day had been going so well too. I got to bottle-feed the cutest black bear cub while his mother was in surgery. She had been injured in one of those inhumane bear traps and her cub never left her side, so when a Fish and Wildlife officer found them, they were both brought to us.

Working in the wildlife division of the vet clinic was my absolute favorite. Not that I didn't love pets too, and was happy to treat the town's dogs and cats when they were brought in, but there was something extra awe-inspiring when working with wild animals. I never knew if I'd be treating a ground squirrel or a gray wolf. A raccoon or a moose. There was never a dull moment in the wildlife division, and I had the privilege of working with animals that most people never got to see up close.

I loved this job. I thought that after years of vet school and disappointing my parents with my life choices, I'd finally found a place I could settle in for a long, fulfilling career.

But all that came crashing down tonight.

I continued to sit in my car, willing my tears to stop so I could drive home somewhat safely.

My phone buzzed from somewhere inside my purse, which was still in my lap. I tossed the whole thing in the footwell of the passenger seat with a defeated sob. It was most likely my mother texting me, and I was in no state to break the news to her now. Not when her smug *'I told you so'* would flash loud and clear through the phone screen, even if she didn't use those exact words.

"God, fuck this." I wiped my eyes for a final time before sticking my key in the ignition.

My decade-old hatchback sputtered to life, headlights lighting up the empty vet clinic parking lot. I didn't have to look up to know that the night staff were probably staring out the window and talking about what'd just happened. And now I looked like a weirdo just sitting in my car, doing nothing.

I blinked and wiped more tears as I pulled out onto the narrow road. Because we worked with Fish and Wildlife and various wildlife rescue groups, the clinic was situated within the boundaries of Plumas National Forest, ten miles outside of Fulsburg. But it was a straight shot into town, so I'd be home to wallow soon. All I had to do was keep my shit together and not run off the road.

My headlights showed the narrow two-lane road in front of me and not much else.

Wilderness still ruled here, and humans were merely guests. When people thought about California, they didn't think about towns like these. Fulsburg was founded as one of many gold rush settlements in the 1850s. When the gold ran dry and most people left to find work in the cities, the wilderness reclaimed the town as its own.

Now, there was no rush of any kind. People chose to live up here because the mountains were beautiful and peaceful. Some, like me, came here to escape.

I also wanted to prove myself. To show that not every choice I made was a colossal fuck-up, that I could make a living doing what I loved and be independent of my parents' expectations. For the last year, up until this evening, I still believed it was possible.

And yet, all I could hear were my parents' voices in my head.

"I'm very sorry to hear it didn't work out like you hoped," came my father's voice, accented by the pouring of his favorite single-malt whiskey into a crystal tumbler. *"But a successful life isn't built on hope and lofty dreams, Emmaline. You need to be pragmatic. We've told you this."*

"You're only twenty-six," my mother would add, fingering her pearl necklace. *"It's not too late to get a* real *medical degree. Or go to law school, perhaps."*

The road in front of me turned into wavy, wobbly shapes, and I swiped at my eyes again. *Fuck.* This meant I'd have to keep my waitressing job at Buck's Peak Bar & Grill. I had been so looking forward to putting in my two weeks' notice tomorrow.

I breathed out a long, shaky breath. "It's not like you got fired," I said aloud in a lame attempt at optimism.

No, I was just staying at my two-day a week schedule, despite being all but promised I'd become a full-time veterinary resident after a year-long internship. I had said yes to the internship offer so fast, easily willing to work a second job if it meant I'd have my dream career in a year.

So stupid.

"If you had taken a single law class, you would have known to have gotten a conditional offer in writing," said my mother's voice in my head. *"You see what happens when you go against our advice? Those little hick towns are so backwards in everything they do. You should have stayed in a proper city."*

I wiped my eyes again just as a huge shape darted in front of my headlights.

"Fuck!" I slammed on the brakes and swerved, but the

impact was unavoidable. My bumper's front left corner hit the animal with a solid thud, and my car went spinning.

As quickly as it happened, it was over.

My car jerked to a halt with a squeal of brakes. Everything was still. No noise or movement. Just darkness, the glow of my headlights, and my ragged breathing.

"Shit, what did I hit?"

Whatever it was had been big and moved fast. Possibly a bear, or even a young moose. That impact had felt solid.

Thankfully, I didn't hit anything else or roll the car or something. My swerve was tight, I'd basically done a U-turn in the middle of the road and was now facing the opposite direction.

With shaking hands, I drove carefully onto the shoulder. That was when I saw it.

My headlights picked up a long, four-legged body lying unmoving on the side of the road. It was covered in gray and black fur, but from this angle I couldn't tell exactly what kind of animal it was. No bear or moose had fur like that. Maybe an elk, but that still didn't seem quite right.

I got out of the car without thinking, leaving my lights on, and hurried over. In hindsight, I probably should have been more concerned for my safety, but my animal-loving heart was bleeding. This was my fault, and if I could fix this, I had to try.

When I reached the animal, I could only stand over it and bring a hand to my mouth. "Oh, God..."

It was a wolf. A huge, beautiful gray wolf, which happened to be my favorite animal. The fact that I possibly just killed one on a day that was already shit-tastic made my heart shatter.

"Oh no, no, no..." I dropped to my knees, my hands

sinking into that dense, warm fur as I leaned over the beautiful animal. "I'm so sorry. Please don't give up on me, okay? Let me fix this."

To my utter relief, he was still breathing, although shallowly. I couldn't get over how huge he was. By my estimation, he was nearly four feet tall at the shoulder and well over two hundred pounds. Definitely the biggest wild wolf I'd ever seen.

I'd hit him on the left flank and most likely broke his thigh bone, possibly even his pelvis, but I'd have to do X-rays to make sure. He must have knocked himself unconscious when he rolled, but he didn't appear to have any other major injuries.

There was absolutely no way I was about to leave this wolf to die. The question was just a matter of how I would take him back to the clinic. By myself, no less.

My hand went to my cell phone in my sweater pocket. I could call someone from the night crew and have them come out to help me, but could I afford to wait? Time was of the essence, and every minute this wolf wasn't receiving care was another minute I could lose him.

He was my responsibility. It was on me to take care of him.

That oddly possessive thought gave me resolve as I strode back to my car. I turned around and backed up as close to the wolf as I dared, then popped my trunk release and got out of the driver's seat.

"Come on, come on..." I prayed silently as I moved a pile of reusable grocery bags and a blanket. "Yes!"

I couldn't remember if I'd removed the ramp from my car or not and thanked my lucky stars that I still had it. A few weeks ago, we'd used it to move a tranquilized mountain lion from the clinic to its wild habitat. With the help of a blanket, it was much easier to move a large animal up and down a ramp rather than lift it straight up from the ground. Which was exactly what I planned to do with the wolf.

All by myself.

I didn't have time to think about how hard it would be, so I set up the ramp, grabbed a blanket, and returned to my wolf's side. The first thing I did was recheck his breathing.

His ribs continued to rise and fall slowly, so I set to work unfolding the blanket.

"Sorry if this hurts, big, uh–," I took a quick peek to check and yep, he was definitely male, "–big guy, but I gotta move you."

I scooped under his hindquarters first and placed his back end on the blanket. "Good boy," I said, not caring how ridiculous I sounded talking to a wild animal like a dog. This wolf would tear my throat out if he was conscious.

I ran back and forth, scooting his hind legs and then his front to move him little by little onto the blanket. After he was fully on it, I had to stop for a few moments to catch my breath. He wasn't just big, he was dense and muscular. Lifting just parts of his body felt like picking up boulders.

"Alright, here we go."

I grabbed the edge of the blanket, dug my heels into the ground, and started pulling him toward my car. "You're lucky I love wolves so much," I grunted, hauling him toward the ramp.

I had to rotate the blanket a few times to ensure he wouldn't fall off the ramp, but after lots more pulling, I finally had him in the trunk of my car.

Physically, the hard part was over, but I couldn't celebrate yet. I had to keep this wolf alive.

After making sure he was secure, I closed up my trunk and got back into the driver's seat.

"There's an actual goddamn wolf in my car."

That was my one moment of bewilderment before I hit the gas and cranked the steering wheel, turning the car around to head back to the vet clinic.

My personal career situation was the furthest thing from my mind at that point. All that mattered was that I went through four years of vet school, plus had on-the-job experience. I had all the skills necessary to save this wolf's life. And that was exactly what I intended to do.

EMMALINE

I lowered my surgical mask and took my first deep breath in hours. The wolf's injuries were not life-threatening, and he was going to make a full recovery.

"I can't thank you two enough," I said to Tori and Michelle, the two vet techs who'd been looking forward to an easy night shift until I'd rushed back to the clinic with an unconscious wolf in my trunk.

"No problem." Tori stuck her hands in the pockets of her scrubs. "Definitely made for an interesting night."

After getting over their initial shock, they'd helped me anesthetize the wolf, X-ray him from head to tail, and perform a full-body exam.

He did have minor head trauma, which likely came directly after the impact, but no major damage to his neck or spine. His rear leg where my bumper had struck him only sustained a hairline fracture. I could hardly believe the X-ray when I saw it and almost had Tori take another image.

His bone density and muscle mass due to his size must have saved him. I had been expecting much worse.

The three of us looked at the wolf sleeping off the anesthesia in our largest dog crate which still barely contained him. He was breathing deeply now, his side rising and falling in a steady cadence.

"Should we call Fish and Wildlife?" Michelle fiddled nervously with her stethoscope. "Wolves don't usually get this close to civilization, right?"

"I mean, it was still miles outside of town. I wouldn't exactly call it close," I said. "Wolf sightings aren't all that unusual."

"Do you think he could be somebody's pet?" Tori wondered. "One of those wolfdog hybrids?"

All three of us trained our gazes on the sleeping animal again. No one needed to say that idea was pretty much impossible. Wolfdogs were usually smaller than pure wolves. This guy was around fifty percent bigger than an average wolf. I found it more likely for him to be a direwolf, an ancestor of modern wolves that were believed to be extinct.

"We got a blood sample, right?" At the techs' nods, I said, "Let's send it out for analysis. That'll be able to tell us if he's crossed with anything or maybe a subspecies we don't usually see in this area."

"Here's a question." Michelle turned to face us. "What do we tell the boss when he comes in?"

I held back my cringe. Dr. Stone, the head veterinarian, was the reason I had left work in tears and feeling like shit. He was the one who decided not to approve my residency application. According to him, the reason was because of budget restraints. However, I had been one of two vet interns. One of us got the residency, and it wasn't me.

Dr. Stone gave me the whole spiel about how it was such a tough decision and it was nothing personal. Considering how I gave everything I had to this job and the other intern, Marcus, called out sick half the time, I found it pretty hard to believe it wasn't personal.

Marcus' family were local big wigs and I'd bet money they were connected to Dr. Stone in some way. Strings got pulled. Favors got called in. It was how people got ahead in life. The same would have been done for me if I had taken the path my parents set out for me.

But I chose my passion over prestige and an easy ladder to success. I'd have to fight for every position I wanted. I had to remember that.

"Tell Dr. Stone the truth," I said. "I hit the wolf with my car and brought him in. Have him call me if he has an issue with it."

I had a gut feeling that Dr. Stone wouldn't approve any overtime pay for bringing the wolf in, and that was fine with me. As long as I had a chance to save the animal, I'd have worked for free.

Now that my wolf was in the clear, I could relax, go home, and get some much needed sleep. But I found myself reluctant to let him out of my sight. A part of me even entertained the idea of rolling out a sleeping bag and spending the night on the floor next to his cage. Sometimes we did that for patients that were unstable and had to be monitored 24/7.

"We got this, Dr. E." Tori seemed to sense my hesitation to leave. "We'll let you know if anything changes."

My smile was weary as I gathered up my things.

"Alright. I'll stop by tomorrow night to see how he's doing. You two have a good night."

"We'll see you, Doc."

My drive home this time was blissfully uneventful. I showered quickly before falling into bed, sleep taking over faster than I expected. That night I dreamed of running through the woods under a full moon, sniffing out prey with a pack, and answering wolf calls with a singing howl.

)))))♦●●●●●(((

I HAD the lunch shift the next day at my other job, Buck's Peak Bar & Grill. Summer was approaching, and I knew we'd be packed with tourists and snowbirds coming up to spend the season in their mountain summer homes. The sad truth was that waitressing paid more than being a vet intern, especially during the busy season. So until I scored a full-time residency, I'd have to hold onto this job to keep the lights on.

Breezing into the break room, I mumbled a quick hello to my co-worker, Annika. She was my favorite person to work with, although I wouldn't call us friends. Despite being night and day different, we got along and worked together efficiently.

"Hey," she greeted, tying up her hair in the mirror. "So, is this it? You putting in your notice today?"

I sighed as I put on my apron. "No. I didn't get the residency."

Annika turned sharply to face me, her long earrings

swinging with the movement. "Aw, dude, I'm sorry. I know you were really excited about it."

"Thanks, it's okay. I'll apply to more places." I forced a smile, figuring I'd tell her the story about the wolf later. "Guess you're stuck with me a little longer."

She turned back to the mirror. "Better you than Betty Biblethumper."

I barely restrained my laugh. "That's mean."

"And her telling me I'm going to Hell isn't? Not that it's not true, but her only intention in saying that is to be a bitch."

One of our coworkers was a deeply religious girl who seemed intent on 'saving' Annika. Conversely, Annika fully embraced an alternative and unconventional style. Not only did she shave the sides of her head, she was covered in tattoos, piercings, and some markings that looked like decorative scars. Rumors had flown through the town that she was a pagan, a satanist, and did ritualistic orgies. She was a culture shock for this small, somewhat conservative town, but didn't seem to care. She did her job and was polite enough to the customers but kept quiet about her personal life.

"For what it's worth, I don't think you're going to Hell," I said. "You look tough, but I bet you're a softie under all that badassery."

Annika chuckled, her eyes brightening. They were an unusual color, a light golden-green. "Guess I need to try harder."

We started our shift and, for the most part, didn't stop until it was time to clock out four hours later. Despite the lunch rush, time felt like it dragged. I kept looking at the clock, counting down the minutes until I'd be able to see the wolf.

Sure, I got attached to patients easily, but this felt different. I chalked it up to guilt, a sense of being responsible for the wolf getting hurt in the first place. Whatever it was, I just couldn't shake the feeling that I *needed* to see him.

Annika and I said our *See ya next time*s and headed in opposite directions to our cars after clocking out. On a whim, I looked over my shoulder and saw her put a cigarette between her lips and light it.

An older couple sitting outside the coffee shop shook their heads disapprovingly as she walked past them. "You'll put yourself in an early grave with those things, young lady," called the man.

"Oh, I'm way ahead of these things." Annika grinned. "Haven't you heard I like being choked during sex?"

I opened my car door just as the couple responded with shocked gasps. That was Annika, biting back when anyone felt the need to comment on her life choices.

I wish I had her attitude, that courageousness that told people to fuck off if they had anything to say about her looks, her vices, or her decisions in life. If she had been my parents' daughter, they would have disowned her immediately and she wouldn't have cared.

But that wasn't me. I was too much of a people-pleaser. My version of rebellion was going to vet school instead pursuing law or a "real" medical degree. Oh no, the horror. And was it actually being rebellious when I was still hoping to make my parents proud? If only it was easier to just not give a fuck.

My spirits lifted a little when I pulled into the vet clinic parking lot. The thought of seeing my wolf awake and alert put a spring in my step. The poor animal would definitely be confused and frightened by waking up injured and in a cage, but I hoped on some level he would understand that we were helping him. Animals had their own wisdom, their own languages. We just had to be patient and listen.

I entered the clinic through the front, like a human client would with their pet. Coming in the back way was an easier option, but there was the risk of running into Dr. Stone. After what he told me yesterday, I had no desire to see him again so quickly.

So, I breezed up to the reception desk and greeted Macy, the office manager.

"Ohhh, Dr. Emmaline," she said in a conspiratorial tone. Much to the chagrin of Dr. Stone, the younger generation of vets often went by first names. "You are in trouble, missy."

"Let me guess, it has to do with the big furry guy that appeared overnight." I went behind the desk and opened a closet to retrieve one of my white doctor's coats. Even if we weren't clocked in and officially on duty, Dr. Stone was a stickler that all interns, residents, and board-certified specialists wear their coats at all times while on the premises.

"Uh, yeah. That might have something to do with it." Macy gave me a pointed look. "Seems you've got a story to tell."

"I'll have to tell it later. Is the boss pissed?"

"He actually didn't come in today." Macy swiveled in her office chair, returning her attention to the computer in front of her. "Dr. Marcus is filling in."

Oh, great. So I'd have to run into the guy who got the job I wanted.

My facial expression must have betrayed what I felt, because Macy gave me a sympathetic look. "I heard. I'm sorry, it should have been you," she whispered.

"That's alright. Can't win 'em all." I schooled my features, putting a smile on. "So the wolf is doing well?" By now, everyone on staff must have seen him or at least heard what happened.

Before she could answer, a long, mournful howl floated down the hallway.

CHAPTER 3

TRYN

Waking up felt like emerging from hibernation. It felt like I'd been asleep for months, my limbs stiff from holding a position for so long. Everything, body and mind, felt like I'd been buried under a thick layer of mud and debris. It was a slow, arduous struggle just to become fully awake.

The first thing I noticed was that I was in wolf form. My keen hearing and nose picked up the strangest noises and smells. Voices and footsteps I didn't know, the hum of machinery that was definitely not my packs' motorcycle engines.

And the smells, *ugh*. I rubbed a paw over my snout. My sensitive nose burned on the inside from all the sharp, astringent chemicals in the air. What was that, cleaning supplies? It became bearable after a few moments only because of other scents hanging in the air. They softened the chemical harshness but weren't strong in themselves. Thank the moon for that. These other scents were unremarkable, neutral, like water or plastic.

My ears pricked, honing in on my surroundings as more awareness filtered in. I knew of only one creature with that simple, neutral scent, and it was alarming that I'd be surrounded by so many of them. In wolf form, no less.

When my eyes could finally focus on what was in front of me, a jolt of panic ran down my spine. A fear-tinged growl loosed from my throat.

"Oh, looks like the wolf's awake," one of the creatures, a human, remarked.

"He doesn't sound happy," someone else added.

Bars. There were bars in front of me, surrounding me on all sides. I was in a fucking cage, in a foreign world.

The human world.

I rose to all fours, or at least tried to. Something was wrong with my back leg. It didn't matter. I couldn't let them see weakness. Another growl rumbled out of my throat, but I was past giving them any warnings. They had me captured, locked up like a pet. If any of them came near, I wouldn't hesitate to strike.

Turning to hide my maimed leg, I made myself as big and imposing as I could. My spine pressed against the top of the cage and my fur puffed out in all directions. I could barely turn around in this thing. If I tried, maybe I could break out, but who knew what these humans were capable of?

There was a reason why our ancestors hid their shifting abilities when they came to the human world to escape the vampires during the war. Humans in our world were the exception, not the rule, and we didn't have many. With billions of humans in this world though, I wasn't ready to trust any of them.

"He is *really* not happy."

Astute observation, human, I thought, snapping my jaws through my growl. *Come closer, I dare you.*

There was a small crowd gathering around my cage. One human male wore a white lab coat that had *Dr. Marcus* embroidered on one side. Another male and two females wore scrubs and ugly shoes with holes all over them.

Fuck, this might be even worse than I thought. Doctors, or scientists, maybe? Did they see me shift and now wanted to run experiments on me? I'd rather run my motorcycle off a cliff before I allowed myself to become a lab rat.

"Easy, boy," one of the women in scrubs said. "We're not gonna hurt you."

She edged toward my cage and I snapped my jaws in her direction, making her flinch and back away.

Don't 'easy boy' me. I'm not your fucking dog, human.

"Alright, never mind." She turned toward her colleagues. "We'll have to fully sedate him to run any tests. It's just not safe otherwise."

Fuck no, you are not sedating me! I growled louder and raked a paw over the linked bars in my cage.

The white-coated man, Dr. Marcus, crossed his arms and furrowed his brow like he disapproved of what I had just done. "What was Dr. E thinking? She knows we don't have resources to spare, especially on a wolf this size. He's gonna need twice a standard dose to knock out."

"She hit him with her car. What was she supposed to do, leave him?"

The doctor shrugged. "I dunno, maybe? We can't save every animal, Justine."

The woman who argued rolled her eyes. "I'm sure Dr. Stone can find room in the budget for one big wolf."

My growling softened as I listened. It didn't sound like

they knew I could shift, which was a relief. It was also news to me that I had been hit by a car.

I remembered running at night, following a trail that kept appearing and disappearing. It wasn't a scent trail but one that was unique to me. Something only I could see, passed down to me from my grandmother, a moon witch.

I had been following a silver thread made of moonlight. A path that I'd hoped would lead me to my fated mate.

Instead, it led me to almost becoming roadkill, apparently. And now in a cage surrounded by humans. I found myself agreeing with the doctor. Whoever had hit me should have just left me there.

"I want a full panel done on him by the end of the week," the doctor said. "Also, call the wolf research center. Tell them we might have a unique subspecies on our hands." He gave me an appraising look. "I have *never* seen one this big before."

Eh, can't say the same for you, I mused. *You're about as average as it gets, Doc.*

The rest of what he said sank in, cold and heavy. Research. A panel, which meant blood tests and sedation. They may not have known I was a shifter yet, but they *were* going to experiment on me.

I was outnumbered, cut off from my pack in a foreign world, injured, caged, and I must have already been drugged at least once. In other words, I was fucked.

A whimper started to leave my mouth before I swallowed it down. I had to keep my head on straight, had to think my way out of this. How long had I been gone? Would my packmates be out tracking my scent trail already? It felt like only a day, but who knew how long I'd been out. I scanned the walls of the room outside my cage for a calendar, but there was none to be seen.

If any wolves were looking for me, there was at least one surefire way to communicate with them.

I didn't think for a second longer before I threw my head back and howled.

"Oh, wow..."

Whatever reactions the humans had were drowned out by my song, the call to my brothers for help. I should have known better than to venture into the human world alone, but when it came to our mates, my kind was especially territorial. I didn't want another male sniffing out the partner that was destined for me, but now that I was caged with no mate in sight, I could have used some damn backup.

I had no idea if my pack could even hear me. There were no windows in this room, so for all I knew, I could have been in a bunker underground. But I had to try, had to sound the alarm just in case any of my packmates were nearby. Had to warn them of danger.

There was commotion all around me, but I paid no mind and kept on howling. A door swung open, the draft of air carrying the scent of a new human who hadn't been here before. But underneath that plain, nothing-special scent was...something else.

It intrigued me enough to the point of pausing my howls so I could focus on sniffing the air.

"Hey, big guy," a soft voice said. "I know this is all really overwhelming, but I promise you're okay."

The voice was feminine, warm and soothing, like a caress through my fur. And that scent. She was definitely human, but I wanted more of that understated sweetness that was so subtle. It was familiar, but I couldn't quite place it.

This new human woman kept her distance like all the others. I wanted her closer, not to lash out with a bite, but to press my nose into the source of that scent. To hear her voice even closer so it would soothe my frazzled nerves.

With a soft whine, I lowered my hackles, my head, and eventually, my belly. Lying on the floor of my cage, I now wanted to appear the opposite of threatening.

"That's a good boy," she said, inching closer. "I know you're scared, but we're just trying to help you."

When she acknowledged my fear, I warmed up to her even more. There was a coldness, a sense of detachment, to these other humans that she didn't have. I was just an animal in a cage to them. But she seemed to understand me.

"Careful, Dr. E," someone said. "He was really aggressive a minute ago."

"I know, I'm watching him."

As she approached my cage, I picked out more details. She too wore a white lab coat. The name stitched on the pocket said Dr. Emmaline. And was that...

I blinked. Squinted. Then let out a soft bark of disbelief.

A single silver thread, as thin and fragile as a spider's web, connected her heart to mine.

My pulse jumped to a furious beat while excited yaps and barks left my mouth, but I didn't care. I'd found her. My fated mate.

I poked my nose through the bars of my cage, reaching for her. And yeah, wow. She was beautiful. Dark hair pulled back in a bun with a few strands coming loose. An oval-shaped face with full cheeks I wanted to lick. Round, dark eyes opened wide as she watched me. Her body under the coat hinted at lush curves that my human side wanted to follow like a winding mountain road on my motorcycle.

The fact that she was human, and from a world that didn't believe in my kind no less, was the furthest thing from my mind at that moment. My mate was here, right in front of me. She didn't know it yet, since no one but me could see fate's threads. But she was mine. And there was no denying that fact.

"Holy shit. Dr. E's the wolf whisperer."

My mate smiled, her warm, dark eyes never leaving me. "Have you guys checked his cast?"

"No, he started growling the moment he woke up. We'll have to sedate him for all exams. He's just too dangerous otherwise."

No. No sedation. You wouldn't do that to me, would you, sweet mate? I dropped my head to my paws, maintaining eye contact with her.

"Look, his tail's wagging! He's like a whole different wolf since she walked in."

"Dr. E's got the magic touch," someone else chuckled.

It's moon magic, not that any of you would understand.

My human tilted her head as she looked me over. She was close enough to touch me now, though she kept her hands in her lap.

"Will you let me look at your back leg without biting me?" she asked. "I don't want to sedate you, but we might have to for our own safety."

I let out a low growl that ended in a frustrated bark. She kept saying *we* to refer to the other humans. I'd never bite her to hurt her, only to leave my claiming mark when the time was right, but I didn't want these other humans anywhere near me.

I wanted us alone. I wanted to shift into a man so we could have an actual conversation. I wanted to learn everything about this woman that fate had chosen for me; her fears, her dreams, everything she loved and hated, all her secrets and her history.

Was she purely human or a latent werewolf like Sawyer's mate, Riley? Latent wolves were descendants of our ancestors who went into hiding in the human world, suppressing their abilities and blending in with the pure humans until their moon magic was forgotten. She smelled human, but if her shifting abilities had been suppressed enough, maybe I wouldn't be able to tell from scent alone.

"Be a good boy for me..." my mate said.

Oh I would be good for her. So, so good.

"...and let me examine your leg. If we don't have any problems, you'll get a nice big bowl of food. If you growl or snap at me, I'm sorry, but we're going to have to sedate you. What do you say, handsome?"

Handsome? Sweet moon above, was she trying to make me fall in love already?

"Why do you talk to him like he'll answer you?" one of the other humans quipped.

My human ignored him, her dark, curious gaze latched onto me.

Because you know I understand, don't you? I thought. *Maybe not consciously, but deep inside your subconscious, you know I'm not just a wolf but part of your destiny.*

All that had to be figured out later. My first priority was getting out of this cage and letting my pack know I wasn't roadkill. Then, when the time was right, I would come back for my human mate.

I let out a soft *whuff*, the best I could do in this form to give my consent for the exam.

She smiled in response and made her way to the side of my cage. The other humans began closing in around her and I growled long and low. She could touch me, but I wouldn't allow anyone else to get close.

Immediately, my human turned around to face her colleagues. "You guys should probably give us some space, maybe even leave the room while I do this."

"What? No way, Emmaline!" Dr. Marcus argued. "We're not leaving you alone with an unsedated wild animal."

"The aggression he's showing is fearful. He still feels cornered, trapped. If there are less people in the room, he might relax a bit."

"Or he might bite you and try to escape."

"I don't think so." She cast a thoughtful look down to me. "It seems he likes me."

"No offense, but this idea is highly unprofessional," Dr. Marcus blustered. "Not to mention against clinic policy."

My mate stiffened, her posture almost shrinking while the other doctor puffed himself up. There was some kind of tension between them that I didn't like.

"If you insist, then stay," she said quietly. "But just one person, and keep to the other side of the room. No need to loom over him, he's been through enough."

The male doctor turned his back to slowly meander to the other side of the room, but I saw his eyes roll. Another growl rattled my throat before I could stop it. My mate was his equal, was she not? They were both doctors here. He should have more respect for her.

The other humans filed out until it was just the three of us. Dr. Douchebag leaned against a counter on the far wall, arms and ankles crossed. But Emmaline, my mate, was at my side and that was all that mattered.

"Good boy. Stay nice and calm for me."

She unlatched a panel on the side of my cage, too small for me to get through but big enough for her arm. I stilled, only my tail thumping back and forth as she reached for me.

"You're keeping weight off this leg, that's good." She traced the hard cast on my rear thigh. My fur had been shaved there and her fingers rasped over my bare skin.

I wanted to reach back and lick those fingers, but she might be afraid I'd bite her. I would not have my mate afraid of me, so I continued to sit still, tail wagging at her touch.

All too soon, she pulled her arm back and closed up the panel. "Very good boy. I'm almost done. Can I check your head now?"

My head stayed right where it was, on my front paws, as she clicked on a pen light. I even flattened my ears back to give her easier access.

"Careful," said the other doctor from across the room.

"I know." Her tone held a tinge of annoyance as she shined the light on top of my head, her gloved finger gently prodding a tender spot. I fought the urge to press up toward her hand, maybe guide those fingers to scratch behind my ears.

"Huh, wow." She kept prodding at my head, fingers smoothing over the short fur on my skull.

"What's up?" Dr. Marcus asked.

"His head injury looks to be completely healed. There

was swelling and contusions here last night, now there's…nothing." Her hand pulled away and the light clicked off. "You're a very lucky wolf, aren't you?"

Now that I've found you, yes.

Shifter healing was apparently unusual in this world, and I wondered how that would affect my captivity. In all likelihood, my leg didn't need a cast anymore either.

Emmaline moved away from my cage and I wanted to whine at the distance between us.

"So, how's he look?" Dr. Marcus asked in a flat tone.

"Good. Extremely healthy." She peeled off her gloves and dropped them into a trash can. "I expect the standard six weeks of limited mobility before the cast comes off."

Six weeks?! Oh, fuck no.

"You know I'm going to have to tell Dr. Stone about your little stunt there." Dr. Marcus made himself sound reluctant but I could smell that he was delighted. "You realize what kind of liability it is to touch a wild animal that hasn't been properly sedated? What if a vet tech gets the same idea and they lose a hand?"

"I'm doing what's best for the patient," Emmaline fired back. "If we keep sedating him, he'll never trust us and just become more aggressive."

"He's a wild animal, he's not supposed to trust us. Humans and wolves are *never* supposed to interact. You get him to trust you, we release him, and then what happens? He approaches a human for food and gets shot in the face."

"I'm not trying to tame him, I just…" Emmaline was flustered, and I would've given anything to shift into a man that could hold her, calm her as she had calmed me.

"Whatever. It doesn't matter," she grumbled. "Tell Dr. Stone whatever you want. It makes no difference to me."

She left the room, and the other doctor followed soon after, but not before I caught the smug smirk on his face. What an asshole. I obviously didn't know the whole story but he seemed like little more than a workplace bully.

Once alone, I turned my attention to the cast on my leg, sniffing it out and testing my teeth against the hard plaster.

I had to get out of here way sooner than six weeks. And for that, I would have to get creative.

Pulling back my lips, I scraped my teeth over the cast and got to work.

CHAPTER 4

EMMALINE

I wanted to visit my wolf as often as I could, especially on my days off, but after Marcus's thinly veiled threat, I thought it might be better to keep my distance.

He wasn't wrong that there were serious liability issues surrounding contact with a wild animal, an apex predator no less, especially if they weren't sedated or under anesthesia. I knew the policy. So did he and everyone else on staff.

Marcus had never cared about following the rules before throwing it in my face. So what'd changed? It didn't take long for me to reach a conclusion.

That asshole wanted me gone.

Whether I left of my own accord or got fired didn't matter. It wasn't enough that he got the residency and I didn't. He still saw me as a threat to his position and wanted me gone for good.

If it had been me informing Marcus that I'd have to tell our boss he violated policy, he'd call me a snitch.

It felt like I held my breath for the next three days, but

no call came from Dr. Stone to lecture me, let me go, or anything else. In order to keep myself from waiting anxiously by the phone, I picked up extra shifts at Buck's Peak and applied to roughly a dozen vet residencies all over the country.

I'd grown attached to this little mountain town, especially working with the wildlife. But if there were no career prospects for me here, I had no choice but to move on. The only place I avoided applying to jobs was my old hometown of Tiburon. Just to be safe, I avoided all of Marin County.

I was still dodging calls and texts from my parents, not wanting to deal with their judgment and *I-told-you-sos*. They knew I was banking on a residency after a year of interning. Time was up. I just knew they were chomping at the bit to hear that I'd been passed over.

Well, I wasn't about to give them the satisfaction.

After those three days off, I showed up early for work at the clinic. The reception area was dark and quiet. Apparently I'd even beaten Macy and was the only one here. Good. That meant a moment of alone time with my wolf.

I turned the lights on and started a pot of coffee in the break room before heading back to see him.

All seemed well at first. The wolf was in his kennel with a water dish and food bowl in the corner. He lifted his head, ears perked and golden eyes alert, when I came through the door.

"Good morning, handsome." I flipped on the lights before approaching his cage. "How are you doing? I missed you."

He rose smoothly to his feet and let out a soft bark of greeting, his tail wagging from side to side.

I couldn't help but smile as I knelt to his level. "I take it you missed me too?"

His tail wagged faster as he licked his lips and let out a short howl.

He was beautiful to look at, the strength and size of him, not to mention his coat pattern and the wild intelligence in those canine eyes. I was so entranced by him that it took me a moment to notice that his leg cast was gone.

"What the hell?" I stared at his shaved flank. The swelling and discoloration of his injury was gone, like he never got hit with my fucking car three days ago. All that remained was a light scar. Even the stitches I'd made were gone.

I took a step back, utterly dumbfounded by what I was seeing. Hairline fractures didn't just heal in three days. The head injury I could chalk up to looking worse than it actually was. But *this* was impossible.

The wolf lowered his head and let out a soft whine, like he was sad that I'd backed away. But no, I couldn't let myself project human emotions onto animals right now. I had to focus. What remained of the cast and sutures were discarded around his paws. The sutures were in pieces, and the cast had frayed, torn edges like it had been chewed off.

I looked at the wolf's face. It *kind of* made sense. Animals often chewed or licked at their injuries because of the discomfort, but not even *he* should have been able to get the entire cast off, let alone the stitches as well. Someone would have seen it and put a cone on him and replaced the cast if necessary.

He had fresh water and bits of leftover food still in his bowl, so he'd definitely been checked on. How had he managed to hide the state of his leg?

The wolf whined again and turned around in a circle, tapping his paws on the kennel floor when he faced me again. It was like he was showing me that he was completely healed. And it was true, he did distribute his weight evenly between all four legs.

The evidence was right in front of me. And still, it was impossible.

"How?" I asked. "How are you good as new after just a few days?"

He sat, again demonstrating that he had full range of motion in both hind legs, and looked at me imploringly, like a dog waiting for a treat.

He was as far away from a domestic canine as a wolf could possibly be. And yet he seemed to almost...defer to me. Waiting for a command like a pet would.

"I don't understand," I said with a shake of my head. "I don't know how to explain any of this at all."

The wolf whined softly again and pawed at the kennel wall, those massive paw pads and claws making the wires bow under the weight of them.

"Of course, you want to be let out." I nodded. "To go back home. You probably have a pack waiting for you, huh?"

He lowered his paw and stuck his nose through the bars.

"I have to get one of the vets to sign off on it. Either Dr. Stone or Dr. Marcus—"

The wolf growled at the mention of those names and I laughed. From a human lens, it would seem this wolf liked me and hated the two of them. Some animals had a good sense about people, but that was a silly thought to entertain.

"They're not gonna believe you healed from a hairline fracture this soon, but as long as I'm not hallucinating and they see what I see," I cocked my head from side to side and the wolf copied the movement, "I don't see any reason why they wouldn't release you."

For some reason, my chest ached at the thought of never seeing this wolf again. True, he'd been the highlight of my week and I loved wolves in general, but I'd never gotten attached to other animals like this one. Something about him was special. Different.

)))))◗◗●◖◖◖◖◖(

A few hours later, I was sitting across the large desk in Dr. Stone's office, which was currently being occupied by my arch nemesis.

"Actually." Dr. Marcus leaned back in the leather office chair, hands clasped behind his head. "I'm thinking we should keep the wolf a little longer."

I stared at him from across the desk, stopping short of jumping up to plant my palms on that lacquered wood and demanding why. But really, what else should I have expected?

"Why?" I asked as politely as I could muster instead.

"We need to run another blood panel on him. The sample you got came back inconclusive." Dr. Marcus gestured at a piece of paper in front of him. "We also have people from the Wolf Research Center coming down to see him for themselves."

"Why?" I asked again, knowing I must have sounded like an annoying child.

He shook his head with a scoff. "You don't get it, Emmaline. This could be an undiscovered wolf species. Do you have any idea how much prestige that comes with? This little backwoods country vet clinic can become something *huge.*"

And you'll become famous, I thought, which was almost certainly the real reason he wanted this.

"If he's a different species, there's more of his kind out there," I pointed out. "We'll send a report to the research center, to Fish and Wildlife, the park rangers, everyone who might get another sighting. But this wolf deserves to be released."

"Deserves?" Marcus repeated in a mocking tone. "Damn, you really are a bleeding heart."

"We're veterinarians," I snapped. "Our duty is to help animals, not use them for prestige and fame."

"Correction." He held up an index finger. "*I* am a resident veterinarian. *You* are just a veterinary intern."

"We both have the same letters after our names, D-V-M," I said. "You're not better than me just because you got the residency."

"Mm, some would argue that I am," he replied smugly.

He wasn't wrong. Some people out there would agree with him. People who believed your entire self-worth was based on your position in society, how high you climbed that ladder and who you rubbed elbows with.

I hated that gut-deep knowledge that my parents were among those people.

In any case, how was I supposed to respond to that? He was being a bully, trying to make me feel small. After a lifetime of being compared to my more successful peers, you'd think I'd learn to not tolerate shots at my self-esteem.

But I wasn't a badass like Annika. I couldn't conjure up a don't-give-a-fuck attitude. The truth was... I did care. Too much. All my life I'd been taught that other people's perception of me was all that mattered. And I always failed to measure up.

That didn't mean I was going to allow my wolf to stay in a cage.

"I only need one vet to sign off on the wolf's release," I said quietly. "If you won't do it, then I'll ask Dr. Stone."

Marcus barked out a laugh. "And you think he'll say yes to you over me?"

I shrugged. "Dr. Stone cares about wildlife conservation."

"He also cares about funding for the clinic. Putting this little town on the map and drawing even more tourists here. Big picture shit. Not just one stupid wolf." Marcus leaned back farther in his chair when I didn't respond. "Anyway, I already talked to Dr. Stone. He's on board with everything I just told you. So you can save your breath, Emmaline. He's not going to release the wolf."

In my mind, I screamed, picked up the coffee cup on his desk and threw it in his face. Demanded for him to do the right thing for the animal, not sacrifice the wolf for funding, prestige, or other stupid reasons. It seemed so completely unfair that he could throw his weight around and I just had to take what was given.

"Okay." I stood from the chair and headed for the office door, not giving him a moment to patronize me any more than he already had. "Thanks for your time, Dr. Marcus."

My decision was made before the door clicked shut

behind me. It had teased the edge of my thoughts since I sat down with Marcus, but after that conversation, I knew it had to be done.

I was going to release the wolf myself.

)))))♦●●(((((

IT WAS SURPRISINGLY EASY. Marcus left work early as usual. Dr. Stone wasn't due to come in today, so as the most senior staff member, I stayed late. Again.

I felt oddly calm, knowing full well what I intended to do. Just a few days ago, the news that I hadn't gotten the full-time resident position nearly broke me. Now, I was almost certainly going to get fired for this. It wasn't that I didn't care, but I felt almost at peace with this decision because it was the right thing to do.

I was already a huge disappointment in the eyes of my family. Why not just toss more failures onto the pile?

And besides, I still had my waitressing job and could always pick up more shifts. Just until I figured something else out.

It wasn't even difficult lying to the vet techs who showed up for the night shift. They had no reason to not believe Dr. Stone had signed off on releasing the wolf.

Before forging his signature on the official document, I practiced it about a dozen times on a piece of scratch paper. Once confident it was good enough, I sent the evidence right through the shredder.

The techs even helped me slide the wolf's kennel across the exam room to the back door. The clinic backed up to a national forest, so we didn't need to transport him anywhere. All we needed to do was open the door and he'd be free.

"Here we go."

I unlatched the largest panel in the front of the cage and slid it up. The wolf darted out with incredible speed, but he didn't go far.

He stopped about fifty feet away and did the most adorable series of stretches. First was downward dog, then he stretched forward and let out a short, happy howl. Then he spun in circles, chasing his wagging tail.

"Oh my God, what a cutie." Tori and Michelle both had their phones out, recording his silly antics. "He's so happy to be out of there."

"Back where he belongs," I agreed, trying to ignore the lump in my throat.

Why did I feel so sad? Of course I was happy to see him uncaged and in good health. But once he took off through those woods, I'd never see him again. And that thought hurt me in a way I didn't expect. It felt like saying goodbye to a close friend moving to a faraway country.

"Aww, look at him!" Tori pointed.

The wolf had flipped to his back, paws in the air and belly to the sky as he twisted back and forth.

"I wish I could pet his belly. He's so fluffy for a wolf," Michelle cooed.

"You can't." The edge of possessiveness in my voice took me and the techs by surprise. Even stranger, I felt it rise up in my chest, a jealous anger that made no sense. They couldn't touch him because he was *my* wolf.

"I mean, it's not safe," I tacked on. "Wolves aren't pets."

"I know that, Dr. E," Michelle said hesitantly. "I was just saying he's a fluffy boy, that's all."

"Yeah. I know, sorry." I rubbed my forehead like the sudden onslaught of emotions was due to a headache. "It's just bittersweet seeing him go."

The wolf had gotten to his feet and started heading toward the treeline. He seemed to be stalling though, sniffing the ground before looking back at us.

"Go on, handsome," I whispered. "Go back to your pack."

He turned to face us and I swore he made direct eye contact with only me. Then he let out a short series of howls and barks before bounding into the forest.

We all stood quietly for a moment, staring at the empty space where he'd just been.

"Well, that was something special." Tori closed the kennel door and started dragging it back inside.

"Definitely gonna miss him." Michelle sighed, closing the clinic door.

That possessiveness reared up in me again, and I had to excuse myself to the bathroom so I wouldn't lash out again.

The only thing that calmed me, as nonsensical as it was, were those howls and barks the wolf made before he left.

It went against everything I knew about humans and animals, but some part of me just *knew* he had spoken to me.

CHAPTER 5
EMMALINE

D r. Stone called me the very next day to, "Discuss matters of my employment," as he put it.

My heart pounded a furious drumbeat, and my hands started to sweat so much that I almost dropped the phone. "Of course, Dr. Stone. I'd be happy to answer any questions you have."

This is it, I thought. *I really am getting fired.*

"Let's not do this over the phone, actually," my boss answered. "Why don't we meet for a drink at your other job?"

I blinked, confused. "At Buck's Peak? Are you sure you want to talk there?"

"Why not? Hear what I have to say and everything might work out."

My heartbeat started to calm while questions raced through my mind. That didn't sound like I was being fired. This could be a good thing. A recommendation to another clinic, maybe? Could it be that he actually *didn't* hold the wolf's release against me?

"Emmaline? Are you still there?"

"Yes! Sorry, Dr. Stone. Um, sure, we can meet at the restaurant. What time sounds good?" It took all my resolve to not shout, *Do I still have a job or not?* But that was unprofessional and Dr. Stone was old-school, a man of decorum.

He didn't strike me as the type to meet with an employee at a restaurant, but that could just be a misread on my part. It was normal for bosses to treat their employees to a meal or drink, right?

We agreed on a time this evening, several hours away. It was a day off for me and I knew I'd go crazy wondering what he wanted to talk about until then. I needed to burn off some energy, calm my nerves.

Five minutes later, I threw on a coat, a beanie, and a pair of hiking boots. It was time to go on a walk.

The great thing about living in a small mountain town was the abundance of nature and walking trails. I set off on the trail next to my apartment, which meandered through dense clusters of trees at times.

It was a bright mid-morning, the air still crisp despite the sunlight. Others were out walking dogs, pushing strollers, or jogging. I stopped to chat with a neighbor of mine walking his Siberian husky.

Petting that dog reminded me of my wolf, even though they were practically night and day different. The husky was maybe half of my wolf's size, not to mention excitable and dopey to the wolf's watchful alertness. But it made me wonder if the wolf had reunited with his pack. If he possibly remembered me, even just as that human who opened his cage and let him free.

Again with the projection of human emotions, I chastised

myself. *Maybe Marcus is right. You have no business being a vet.*

I followed the trail until the loop completed, trying to keep the negative thoughts at bay. I was crossing through the last copse of trees before reaching my apartment when I heard it.

A growl.

I whipped around, scanning the trees. A twig cracked and I spun again. Was that a four-legged animal I saw slinking away at the edge of my vision? It was impossible to be sure.

For a moment, I stood frozen, just feet away from my front door. Nothing moved, and I didn't hear anything else. I thought about going toward the noise to investigate but that was dumb, not to mention dangerous.

But if an animal was injured...

Scoffing at myself, I headed to my apartment. Who was I kidding? My dumbass had actually hoped it was the wolf coming to see me again. Which was so deluded, it was embarrassing. He was a wild animal. Not a lost dog that had grown attached to me.

The sooner I realized that, the better.

SIX HOURS LATER, I walked through the front doors of Buck's Peak Bar & Grill, a few minutes early for my meeting with Dr. Stone. My attire was the epitome of business casual, a blazer over a simple blouse, my nicest straight-legged jeans, and ankle boots with a low, chunky heel.

I didn't want to overdress for a casual setting, but figured I should still look polished and professional if there was any chance of keeping my job.

"Hey, Emmaline," Joey, the bartender , greeted me. "You're not working tonight, are you?"

"No, I'm meeting someone." I slid into the middle stool at the currently-empty bar.

"Ah, hot date?"

"No!" I laughed. "It's actually with my boss at my vet job. He wanted to talk about work stuff."

"Alright, I gotcha. Well can I get anything started for ya?"

I pondered for a moment. "I'll take an Irish red, just a half-pour." The nerves had returned and a small drink would definitely help take the edge off without impairing me.

"Coming right up."

"Thanks, Joey."

He had just set my beer in front of me when the deep growl of a rumbling engine approached the restaurant. It grew close enough to vibrate the floor and bartop before cutting off abruptly.

"That's a sweet bike," Joey murmured appreciatively.

I wasn't a motorcycle aficionado by any means, so didn't bother turning to look. We got bikers rolling through town pretty regularly and they often stopped at Buck's Peak. In my experience, motorcycle clubs were in one of two camps. Either they kept to themselves or they intended to start trouble. When you were a waitress or bartender, you always hoped for the former.

I wasn't even on duty and I was crossing my fingers that this guy wouldn't cause problems for my coworkers.

"How's it going?" Joey greeted the biker who came in and headed for the bar on heavy, lumbering footsteps.

"I'm alright. How 'bout yourself?"

Whoa. I did not expect a voice like that. Deep, silky and rich, with just a touch of roughness to it.

When the biker reached the bar, his presence loomed huge and imposing to my right side. I glanced over and saw huge hands gripping the back of a barstool. Those hands led up to thick, muscled forearms, and then even bigger biceps and shoulders.

"Ah, I'm good. Thanks." Joey seemed equally flustered by this biker. "What can I get you?"

"Hmm. What's good here?"

One those huge hands lifted up, and my gaze followed the movement. He stroked a short beard neatly trimmed around his jaw and full lips. The lines of his jaw and nose were sharp. What surprised me the most was his hair. It was a rich, dark brown falling in careless waves to his shoulders, and it looked *so* soft.

Joey was rattling on about our drink menu, none of which registered until he said my name.

"And Emmaline here's got our local Irish red."

"Really?" the biker rumbled in casual but sincere interest. "That sounds great."

All of a sudden that face turned towards me, and I was met with the most beautiful golden-brown eyes I'd ever seen.

"Uh, yeah!" I smiled too wide and bobbed my head like an idiot, probably. "It's really good. Highly recommend it."

I gulped down a breath and, just as I thought this man couldn't get any more stunning, he smiled. "Alright, then. I'll have what she's having."

"Full pour?"

"Please."

Please? This beast of a man was actually polite and knew his manners too? I had to be hallucinating because this could not be real.

"Is anyone sitting here?" His gaze flicked down the barstool he still gripped with one hand. That one subtle movement showed that he had long, full eyelashes as well.

"Uh, nope. Well, you are now."

Oh my God, kill me right this second.

He flashed a crooked smile as he slid smoothly into the seat. For some reason, he seemed even bigger when sitting down. "Thanks. Emmaline, was it?"

"Uh, yep. That's me." I really needed to stop saying "uh" like an idiot. Or even better, stop talking to him altogether.

"I'm Tryn." Joey placed the beer in front of him and he lifted the glass, still smiling. "Thanks for the beer recommendation."

"Uh—sure. Hope you like it."

Tryn took his first sip, and like a damn pervert, I watched his throat bob as he swallowed.

"Damn. That is good." He took one more drink before setting it down. "Gonna have to get some of that back home."

"Where are you from?" So much for no more talking.

"A little mountain community kind of like this one. It's pretty far away, though. What about you? Are you local?"

I had to rush past the fact that this man was actually asking about me like he was really interested so as to not sound like an idiot when I answered. "Oh, I don't think I count as a local yet. I moved here about a year ago for work. I'm from the Bay Area originally."

"Oh yeah? Big city girl, huh?" Tryn smiled at me over the rim of his drink.

"Not really." I chuckled. "I love it up here, actually. I love that it's quiet, scenic, and all the wilderness you could want right on your doorstep."

"Agreed on all fronts. It's a nice town. Never been much of a city guy myself." Tryn was facing me, turned sideways in his barstool. Despite his size, it didn't at all feel like he was encroaching on my personal space. If anything, he seemed to be hanging back to give me even more space.

"What do you do for work out here?" he asked.

Somebody pinch me because he's still *asking questions.* "I'm a vet. Well, a vet intern. I'm actually meeting my boss here. He runs the animal clinic in town." I checked my watch. Dr. Stone must have been running late.

"Oh, well don't let me keep you."

"No, you're fine. He's not here yet." I had gone from mortified and awkward to Miss Social Butterfly, apparently. Hopefully Dr. Stone would continue to take his sweet time so I could talk to Tryn some more. "What do you do for work?"

"I'm a…" Tryn stroked his jaw again, his gaze flicking over the bartop in a way that almost seemed nervous. "It's a bit hard to explain but can be summed up to personal security. I'm with a team of bodyguards for someone important."

"Really?" I found myself leaning toward him, fascinated. "Like a celebrity?"

"Mm, of sorts, but not exactly. For privacy reasons, I can't give out too many details."

"No, of course. I understand. How interesting, though.

Is that job dangerous?" I wanted to play it cool and *not* fawn over this man, but couldn't seem to help myself.

"Yes," he said without hesitation, his face the most serious I'd seen since he walked in. "This, ah, person has enemies. As does everyone associated with them. My team and I are a very close-knit group, though. We're like a family." He smiled again. "A pack, if you will."

"I understand you can't talk about it, but wow. The more you say, the more curious I get."

Tryn took a contemplative sip of his beer. "Well, it's possible I can tell you more."

"What do I have to do?" Oh God, was that flirting? Who the hell was I? "Will you swear me to secrecy? Because I'll do it."

"No, nothing like that." Tryn's smile was almost bashful now and it was so endearing to see on such a huge, tough-looking man. "Just, you know. Spending time like this, getting to know each other." His eyes met mine. "Learning to trust each other."

Before I could respond or even process what he'd said, the front door swung open, bringing a draft inside.

"Sorry I'm late, Emmaline. Hope you weren't waiting long."

Dr. Stone came up and grabbed a barstool on the opposite side of me. He was in his sixties or so, with a shaved head, glasses, and a gray mustache. My boss was also one of those older white guys with a piercing through one earlobe, and I still wasn't sure what to make of that.

"Oh no, not at all." I tried not to sound too disappointed as I shot Tryn an apologetic smile. "It was nice meeting you, Tryn."

"You as well, Emmaline."

With a small smile, he turned to face the bar and I looked down the opposite way toward Dr. Stone, who ended up picking the very last seat at the end.

"Come this way, Emmaline, so we have some privacy."

I slid off of my stool reluctantly, moving away from the hot biker who *might* have been flirting with me. "Do you want to grab a table?"

"No, this is fine. Excuse me, sir?" He leaned over the bar and waved at Joey. "Can I get a martini, please? And put her drinks on my tab." Dr. Stone eyed my half-finished half-glass of beer. "Are you going to have another?"

"No, I don't think so."

"Go on, Emmaline. Have another drink." His mustache twitched when he grinned. "I'll catch up to you soon."

"I'll think about it when I finish this one."

"Ah, come on girl, live a little."

I had never interacted with Dr. Stone outside of work. He seemed so stiff and formal at the clinic. The phrase "professional distance" was an understatement when it came to him. He barely interacted with anyone if it wasn't necessary. This side of him, encouraging me to drink, seemed like a totally different person.

"I'm good for now, thank you," I said with my politest smile. "What did you want to talk to me about?"

His smile dropped as if disappointed. "Okay, then. Straight to business it is." Joey placed his martini in front of him, and after a sip of his drink, Dr. Stone gave me a solemn look. "Look, Emmaline. You're a more-than-capable vet. You've busted your ass, and the clinic has thrived since you've started. Anyone can see how passionate and hard-working you are."

"Um, thank you." I shifted nervously in my seat. All of

that sounded like high praise to me. So he was either softening me up before firing me, or he really was about to give me good news.

"I've spoken with the board and they've agreed that we need more vets on staff. So I talked them into rearranging the budget for us to employ another resident."

My heart drummed wildly, and I could hardly breathe. This was better news than I ever imagined. "Are you serious?"

Dr. Stone smiled, something gleaming in his eyes. "You're our top candidate, naturally. But seeing as the hiring is up to me, I have some...conditions."

I nodded, swallowing nervously. Here was where he was going to lay into me about releasing the wolf, on top of refusing to sedate said wolf. I'd take whatever consequences there were—reduced pay, anything. Considering forging a signature was illegal and he was offering me a job instead of filing a police report, I was thanking all my lucky stars right then.

That was until Dr. Stone placed his hand on my knee.

And kept it there.

"We'll have to be discreet." He lowered his voice to a whisper, leaning entirely too close to me. "No one at the office can know. But give me this," he gave my knee a small squeeze and bile rose up in my throat, "and all the trouble you've caused in the past week will disappear. Plus, you'll be in charge of the clinic when I'm not there."

I was struck dumb by what was happening, what I was hearing. He was so close to me, I could feel his breath on my cheek. And he would not let go of my fucking leg.

"What about your wife?" I managed to stammer.

The other Dr. Stone, this pervert's wife, was considered

a hero in the vet community. Technically, both husband and wife owned the clinic, but she was always traveling with different nonprofit groups that did huge animal rescue operations. Last I heard, she was overseas somewhere helping dogs that were saved from a meat farm.

Meanwhile, her husband scoffed dismissively before taking another drink. "You know how it is. She's never around. It gets lonely sometimes."

Up until now, I was disbelieving almost to the point of disassociation. But reality hit me then, as solid as this disgusting man's hand on my leg.

"Dr. Stone." I forced my voice to not shake and tried to inject all of my will into my words. "I am not sleeping with you. Not for a job or any reason."

"Oh, come on." He huffed like I was the one being ridiculous. "Stacey's had affairs, I've had my fair share of 'em. It's not a big deal."

"Get your hand off me." I shoved his hand away and swung my legs to the side as I slid out of the barstool.

Just then, I felt a huge looming presence at my back, and Dr. Stone's eyes went wide. His gaze traveled up, way over my head.

Behind me, Tryn growled. "She told you no. So get the fuck out of here before you don't have hands to touch anyone with."

CHAPTER 6

EMMALINE

Dr. Stone scowled at the threat, but Tryn didn't back down. If anything, he loomed closer. He didn't touch me, but I felt the bank of heat from his body against my back.

If I were him, I wouldn't be threatened by Dr. Stone's look either. It was like a terrier staring down a wolf.

"You must not be from around here," my boss blustered. "If you were, you'd know better than to threaten me. Do you know who I am?"

"I don't give a fuck who you are," the biker said coolly. "You're being a creep, making this woman uncomfortable, so you need to leave."

Dr. Stone's gaze fell to me and narrowed. "Who is he to you? Did you plan for him to be here?"

"You're done talking to her. Your business is with me," Tryn snarled before I could stammer out a response. "Last chance to leave before I haul you out of here myself."

The two men stayed frozen in some kind of stand-off for a long stretch of time. Finally, Dr. Stone folded.

"Ridiculous," he scoffed, grabbing his coat off the back of his barstool. As he headed toward the door, he looked at me. "You can forget all about that job offer. Or any job with me. Don't bother showing your face at my clinic again."

Just like that, he was gone. I didn't realize the whole restaurant had gone quiet until the atmosphere breathed with ambient noise again. Silverware and glasses clinked and the murmurs of multiple conversations picked up again.

Shit, everyone must have seen and heard that confrontation.

"Are you okay?"

A soft touch landed on my shoulder, prompting me to turn around. Tryn's brow was furrowed with genuine concern, though his amber eyes were still heated with anger. He stepped back, no longer looming over me.

"Can I get a glass of water for her, please?" I heard him ask Joey. Then I was gently led by a large hand back to my original barstool, next to his. "Do you want to sit down?"

I sat, the movement stiff like a robot. The shock was beginning to wear off, but I was still reeling. Dr. Stone wanted me to *have sex with him* for a job. What the fuck?

"Here, Emmy."

The nickname brought my attention back to the present. Joey had set a glass of water in front of me, his brow furrowed and mouth pressed in a hard line, much like Tryn's.

"Thanks." I gulped the water down, not realizing how dry my throat had become. The cool hydration was soothing, easing my nerves a bit. I was safe now, among friends.

"Take deep breaths. You're alright," Tryn rumbled next to me.

He gazed intently at me, like he never wanted me out of his sight. But it wasn't a creepy leer like how Dr. Stone had looked at me. I could almost *feel* that he wanted to keep me safe. Shit, if he hadn't been here...

"Thank you." My voice shook a little. "You didn't have to get involved, but I'm really glad you did."

"Of course I had to get involved." Tryn's lip curled like he wanted to bare his teeth. "I could sme—tell that you were getting uncomfortable, and that asshole just didn't care. What a fucking perv."

I looked at the opposite end of the bar where Dr. Stone and I had sat, and then back at Tryn. "You heard what he said?"

Tryn gave a lopsided smile and a half shrug. "I have good hearing." With a glance at Joey, he added, "Wish I could be sorry I caused a scene but I'm really not. That piece of shit needed to be called out publicly."

"It's all good. He's a big wig in this town." Joey frowned at the front door. "Maybe this'll take him down a few pegs since so many people saw."

"He obviously sucks, but I don't want anything to happen to the clinic." I chewed my lip nervously. "They do good work there." Conflicted feelings swirled within me. Obviously, I didn't want to work for Dr. Stone anymore, but I would miss the actual work, the day-to-day adventures with the animals.

"I'm really sorry about your job," Tryn offered gently. "That's fucked up what he just did. Can you report him to anyone?"

I sighed. "I'm sure I can. I just...don't want to think about all that right now. The staff will surely ask questions, and rumors are going to fly. He might get a lawyer. Damn, *I* might need a lawyer."

"Tomorrow's problems," Tryn said. "Right now, you're away from him and not being manipulated into any gross bullshit."

I smiled. "Thanks to you."

He smiled back and my heart flipped. "Right time, right place, I guess."

"We'll help you out however we can too," Joey said. "Lynn and Buck will understand. They'll give you all the extra shifts you want, I'm sure."

"Thanks, Joey. That means a lot." In so many ways, my serving job was more supportive than the one I paid thousands of dollars and years of schooling for.

Tryn gave me a curious look. "You work here too?"

"Yeah, I never got a chance to tell you that. My vet internship was only part-time hours, so I waitress here to fill in the gaps." I downed the rest of my water and then my beer. "Guess I'm about to be the most overeducated full-time waitress in Fulsburg."

"Well, I know we've only just met, but from what I do know about you," Tryn leaned back and folded his arms, "you're hard working, kind, honest, smart, and you have a lot of integrity. You'll land back on your feet in no time, Emmaline."

His praise hit me in an unexpectedly deep and tender spot. No one had ever said anything resembling those words to me, and I hadn't realized how much I craved them until now. My parents were always disappointed in me, and the cursory "*Congratulations on all your hard work*" from my professors had been about my academic achievements, not about me as a person.

Tryn was a complete stranger, but he saw me as worthy and valuable. A tiny, shallow part of me felt a sting that he didn't include pretty or beautiful in those compliments, but that might have been asking for too much. He was a stunning man, on top of being a total gentleman. He probably had an equally gorgeous wife at home and knew that calling another woman pretty wasn't appropriate. What a lucky wife.

"And now I've made things awkward." He chuckled lightly, bringing his beer to his lips. "Forget I said anything."

"No, you didn't!" I shook my head emphatically at him. "I was just speechless. That's very...nice of you to say."

I was the one making things awkward, projecting so much of my personal shit onto the words he used when he was just trying to cheer me up. It didn't mean anything more than that, and besides, he was definitely, most likely married.

My gaze dropped to his left hand, loosely circled around the base of his pint glass. No ring or ring-shaped tan line, but that didn't necessarily mean anything. Some guys just didn't like jewelry. And Tryn, with his motorcycle, faded jeans, long hair, and overgrown scruff, seemed like the opposite of a jewelry guy.

He seemed rough, a little wild. Like the forest, he was beautiful to look at but could be dangerous if you ventured too deep with knowing your way.

I had no doubt he would have hurt Dr. Stone if pressed. Oddly enough, I wasn't bothered by that. I was more...flattered.

Joey took my now-empty half-pint and set it in a dish-washing tray. "Anything else, Emmy?"

"Actually, yeah. I'll take a full pour this time."

The bartender grinned. "Atta girl. Fuck that pervy old doctor."

"I'll have another too." Tryn set his empty on the edge of the bar and gave me a small smile. "If that's alright with you."

"Sure it is." My casual tone didn't betray how my belly flipped. "I'll get this one for you."

"No." His expression turned stern as he shook his head. "Absolutely not."

"Come on. It's the least I can do for you coming to my rescue."

"Any decent person would have done the same. Plus, I'm buying your drinks."

I laughed. "What? No, you're not."

"You've had a rough day. You deserve it." He angled his head toward Joey. "Doesn't she?"

"I'd say so." Joey set our beers in front of us. "But you're both wrong, 'cause your drinks are on me." Tryn and I started to argue, but Joey whistled loudly, drowning us out as he walked away to help someone else.

"Well, he's getting a hell of a tip." Tryn sat back, chuckling. "Seems like a good dude."

"He is," I agreed. "He trained me when I first started. I'd never had a service job before, and Joey was really sweet and patient with me."

Tryn's eyebrows went up in amusement. "Really? No flipping burgers during high school or anything like that?"

"No, I, um..." My nerves crept back in, as they always did when I talked about my life from before vet school. How was I supposed to explain that my parents believed service jobs were for lowlifes? If they knew I was a waitress now, they'd die of shame on the spot.

"I just really wanted to focus on school," I said to Tryn.

He nodded at that. "You were a good student, I take it?"

It wasn't like I had a choice. "I guess so. I got good grades and was in honors classes. I spent most of my free time studying. So you could say I was a textbook nerd."

"Smarty-pants," Tryn teased.

I chuckled through a sip of beer. "I don't think education is really a measure of intelligence, though. I was good at taking tests, but I wouldn't say I was smarter than a lot of people. All those study habits helped me in vet school, though. So I'm grateful for that."

"I'm sure you're a great vet," Tryn said softly. "Not just because you're good at tests and studying."

"What makes you think that?" The beer was loosening me up, and I felt myself growing bolder. Maybe even flirtatious.

"I'm good at reading people."

"Does that help you in your job?" I asked. "While you're bodyguarding your mysterious important person."

Tryn's smile was full of teeth. "It does, actually."

He didn't elaborate, and even though I was morbidly curious, I didn't pry. I was afraid I might annoy him if I asked too many questions about his job, and I wanted him to stay open and candid with me.

"What about you, were you a good student?" I asked instead.

"No," he said with a sharp laugh. "No, I was one hell of a prankster and drove my teachers mad. Me and my buddy Sawyer, who's basically my brother, would always get into trouble. We got nipped and scruffed so many times."

I squinted at him. "You got...what?"

"Oh, uh, it's an expression where I'm from. Basically we got...yelled at. And thrown out of class."

"Where are you from that has expressions like that?"

He smirked at me over his glass. "Guess."

"Hmm..." He did have a slight accent that I couldn't quite place. It didn't sound anywhere southern or midwestern US, but not quite European either.

I took a stab in the dark. "Canada?"

Tryn laughed. "Holy shit, first guess. I'm that easy, huh?"

"Seriously?" I gaped at him. "I got it right?"

"You sure did." He tapped his glass against mine. "Told you you were smart."

My face heated and I tried not to show how much the compliment affected me. "What part of Canada?"

"Ah, just a little town in the middle of nowhere wilderness. It's not even on most maps."

"What's it called?"

He hesitated for a moment. "Vargmore."

"Vargmore," I repeated. "That sounds so Gothic and mysterious. Like something out of an Edgar Allen Poe story."

Tryn smiled. "I don't know about Gothic, but it is pretty mysterious. We're kind of isolated up there, cut off from the rest of the world. Some families can trace their lineage back thousands of years. We have unique lore, folk tales, and traditions." His eyes flashed with mischief. "You could say my people and I are slightly feral."

"That sounds amazing, honestly." I sighed. "Being close to wilderness is part of why I love it up here so much. The hustle and bustle of cities, all the unspoken rules of society, it's too chaotic for me. Wilderness takes its time. It's quiet and doesn't judge you based on how big your house is or what school you went to. A small, close-knit community that understands that sounds wonderful." A sense of longing filled up my chest, like I was homesick for a place I'd never been to before.

Tryn's expression jerked me out of my daydream of his quiet, hidden community. He looked shocked, eyes wide and lips parted.

Embarrassment prickled over my skin. "Sorry, I didn't mean to ramble." I curled into myself, hiding behind a sip of beer.

"No, don't be. You didn't ramble, it's just…" He seemed lost for words, raking a hand back through his hair before continuing. "It's just uncanny you said all that because it's absolutely true of Vargmore. We have a…special relationship with the wilderness. It's almost a magical connection, or a spiritual one. And yes, we're a very close-knit community that doesn't care about symbols of status or wealth." He gave me a reassuring smile. "I was just surprised you were so right on the nose. You sure you haven't been there?"

"If I had, I'd probably never leave," I admitted. "It sounds wonderful."

"It is. It's home," he murmured.

Home was a foreign concept to me. In all my twenty-six years, I had yet to experience the warmth and sense of belonging that word entailed. My parents' place growing up was cold, clinical. It was a beautiful, custom-built house, but it was far from a home. Since moving out for college, I'd slummed it in dorms and cheap apartments. As much as I enjoyed the town of Fulsburg, my little apartment felt temporary, a transitional place. I wouldn't be staying there forever, especially not if I landed a vet position somewhere else.

I was envious that Tryn had a place he considered home. One that sounded that perfect for me. I almost asked if I could come for a visit, but that seemed an awfully presumptuous question for someone I just met.

"Do they need any veterinarians out there?" I asked with a smirk. When in doubt, bury your actual question under the veil of a joke.

"Maybe," he mused. "You ever work on wild animals?"

"Yes!" I couldn't keep the excitement out of my voice. "I love working on wildlife. We actually just released a wolf who'd been injured. God, he was huge and just *so* beautiful. Bright golden eyes, luscious thick fur, and such a gorgeous coat pattern. I was sad to let him go, but it was what he needed." I conveniently left out all the details about the wolf's super fast healing, my hitting him with my car, or forging my boss's signature to release him. Whether he was married or not, I didn't want Tryn to think less of me.

"That's so cool. You really like wolves, huh?" His voice was warm, if even affectionate.

"Yeah." I gave him a dreamy smile. "They're my absolute favorite animal, if I had to pick."

Tryn looked pleased with that answer, a heart-stopping smile spreading slowly across his lips. "Mine too."

"We have so much in common." It meant to come out as a joke, but my heart beat a little faster when I said it.

I really enjoyed talking with Tryn, felt safe and comfortable with him, and we seemed to be kindred spirits in a way. My day could have turned out horribly, but he turned it all around just by being here.

He polished off the rest of his beer and set the empty on

the far side of the bar. When Joey asked if he wanted another, he shook his head. Our night was coming to an end, and I couldn't help but feel a flicker of sadness.

I put some cash on the bar as a tip for Joey while Tryn did the same, then excused myself to the ladies room. When I got back, Tryn was already standing as though he were about to leave.

"Hey listen, Emmaline." He slid a folded napkin across the bartop toward me and my pulse skyrocketed. "I know you've had a rough day and have a lot going on in general. But I loved talking to you tonight, so that's my number if you'd like to keep in touch."

"Oh, sure! Thanks." I took the napkin and slid it into my pocket, all the while yelling at myself to be cool and not weird. "I had fun talking to you too. And thank you again for helping me out earlier."

"My pleasure." His voice was low, almost sultry. "I'll see you around, hopefully."

"Yeah. Have a good night, Tryn."

"You too."

He said a final goodbye to Joey, then turned and left.

I stood there for a good minute, if not longer, wondering if any of that really happened. Only when the roaring of Tryn's motorcycle faded in the distance did I pull out the napkin to look at his phone number.

My heart sank with crushing disappointment at what I saw.

He'd only written down six digits.

CHAPTER 7

TRYN

I lifted my phone from the table and frowned at the screen. Just to make sure I didn't miss anything, I went to the call records section. Nope, nothing. Voicemail was empty too. The same as it was five minutes ago.

Setting the phone down, I tried to let my surroundings distract me. After giving Emmaline my number, I was back in Vargmore, sitting in the Stout & Spirit tavern with my packmates.

As wolves, we were Howling Death, the ruling pack of the werewolf territory. In our human forms, we fancied ourselves a motorcycle club. Still Howling Death, just with an MC attached to the name.

Ruse, the alpha's second and vice president, knocked his shoulder into mine. "Why the hell are you checking your phone so much?"

I shrugged, resisting the urge to check it again. "Just thought she'd call by now."

It had been three days since I last saw Emmaline, four

since she released me. Our fate thread constantly tugged at my chest, a tether always pulling and urging me to be near her. Once werewolves found their fated mates, it was a constant struggle to be away from them, as I was quickly finding out. No wonder my two mated packmates, Sawyer and Orson, had gone batshit when their females were in danger.

When can we go back? my wolf repeatedly asked me like a child. *When can we see our mate again?*

I had no answer for him, and that only made him antsier.

The last few days had been busy with pack business, plus I didn't want to overwhelm Emmaline. She probably wasn't crazy about male attention after her boss had been such a creep.

I purposely didn't ask for her number so she wouldn't feel pressured, especially after *that* incident. I'd given her mine instead, to leave the ball in her court. The whole time we talked, I tried to scent her emotions as discreetly as I could. She'd been obviously rattled by her boss coming on to her, but I sensed no additional discomfort or fear while she sat next to me. If anything, I thought I picked up disappointment from her when I had to leave.

"Can humans even call our phones from their world?" Ruse asked. "How would that work?"

"Both phones would need a strong signal, but yes, it's possible," Orson cut in. "Some of their cell phone towers actually straddle borders between our worlds. So our devices sometimes ping off of them too. I'm sure their cell companies write them off as anomalies."

Ruse's head swiveled toward. "How do you know that? Actually, never mind."

He answered anyway. "Shiloh and I had the day off, so we decided to try mapping out all the entrances to the human world."

Orson was the tech and finance wizard of the pack and full of knowledge that went over most of our heads. However, what he had in IQ points, he lacked in social skills. With some pushing from me, along with a meddlesome dragon shifter, he'd successfully gotten together with his fated mate. Shiloh was a witch of Vargmore and the owner of Stout & Spirit, the fine establishment we currently sat in.

"Well, did you find them all?" The question came from Fallon with a toothy grin.

While he was a fellow werewolf, Fallon was technically no longer part of the Howling Death pack. He'd become known as the Traveler and was a sort of mediator between all worlds. Not just us and the humans, but also the vampires, dragon shifters, and angels. I didn't know how he did it, but he was somehow the only werewolf freely able to travel to the vampire territory of Sanguine and their allies, the dragons.

His mate, Aria, playfully slapped his arm. "Don't taunt them."

"No." Orson leveled his icy blue stare at the other wolf. "Care to do any sharing in that regard?"

"Nah, I like watching you all chase your tails."

That earned another smack from Aria and grumbling from Orson.

"Answer me this, Ice Man," Ruse said. "Would Tryn know if his human had attempted to reach him even if she wasn't in a prime signal area?"

Orson rolled his eyes at the nickname but proceeded to

answer. "It depends. Texts and voicemails will go through once the signal is strong enough. But if she called, couldn't get through, and didn't leave a message, probably not."

That gave me a little hope. Emmaline may have tried calling, but it just hadn't gone through, so I didn't receive a notification.

"Why don't you just call her instead of sitting around waiting?" Ruse asked. "I know it's a new age and everything, but we're wolves. We go after our mates."

"Says the wolf who doesn't have one," cracked Derric, our Alpha and MC president, from behind his drink.

"Hey, you're one to talk," Ruse shot back. As the VP and second in command, he was one of the few who could get away with talking back to Derric. "You're a single pringle like me, and better for it."

"Eh." Derric made a noise like he wasn't sure about that last part.

"No, Derric. I need you." Ruse whined dramatically. "Stay single in solidarity with me while all these guys are getting mated up."

"That depends on what Tryn sees, I guess." Derric looked at me with a raised eyebrow, referring to my ability to see fate threads and other phenomena that others couldn't.

I grinned at the two of them. "Sorry, guys. Both of your fate threads are as clear as ever, reaching out through the walls. Your mates are out there somewhere."

"Son of a bitch," Ruse grumbled.

It was true. Ruse's thread stretched from his heart toward the center of town. His mate could be anyone in the territory, from someone in our community to a wolf in one of the feral packs living deep in the mountains.

Derric's thread pointed in the opposite direction, roughly toward one of the few entrances to the human world like mine had. Maybe his mate was like Emmaline, a human, possibly a latent wolf who had no awareness of their heritage.

The Alpha didn't seem to care one way or another. He scoffed at Ruse's grumbling before turning his attention to me. "Ruse has a point though. Why don't you reach out to her?"

"I never got her number," I admitted. "Some guy had been bothering her and I stepped in. She was pretty shaken by it, and I didn't want to make her even more uncomfortable. So I figured I'd let her decide if she wanted to see me again."

Ruse snorted. "And I thought Orson was the most clueless werewolf I'd ever seen."

Orson growled. "Fuck you."

"Stop it," Derric snapped. "Both of you."

"No dog fights in my bar, please," Shiloh called out pleasantly.

"Being werewolves doesn't make us cavemen," I said when the two of them put their hackles down. "I'm not going to club her over the head and carry her to my lair."

"I'm not saying that." Ruse turned toward me. "Just don't be so...passive. Don't make her uncomfortable, of course, but make your interest clear. Unquestionable. Make her know that she's yours and yours alone."

"Hang on." Aria lifted a hand. "Humans don't have mates like we do. It's not so cut and dry for them, and sometimes they date multiple people at once. I don't think Tryn is wrong for doing a less aggressive approach, especially just after she encountered a creep. What do you say, Riley?"

If anyone knew human culture well enough to speak on it, it was Riley and Aria. They had both been raised in the human world, not knowing they were latent werewolves until they met their mates.

Riley and Sawyer were on a couch next to our table. She sat normally, while Sawyer stretched out long, his legs dangling over the couch's arm with his head in her lap. The Howling Death enforcer caressed his mate's belly with one hand. Riley wasn't even showing yet, but Sawyer was already enamored with his future pup.

Riley thought for a moment, her fingers curling in Sawyer's hair as she massaged his scalp. "That's true. A lot of humans date casually and prefer low-pressure situations. But there's also plenty of women who appreciate a man taking charge. If she's into him, she'll find it confident and sexy."

I groaned. "That's the opposite of what Aria just said."

The two women laughed.

"I'm glad you find my confusion funny," I grumbled.

"Human women are not all the same." Riley's finger twirled around the streak of silver in Sawyer's hair. "We—I mean, they, all like different things. Different ways to be approached by potential partners. You'll just have to find out what your mate likes."

I nodded, my thoughts filing through what I'd learned about Emmaline when we talked. She liked wilderness and wild animals, especially wolves. She had good taste in beer.

"You could try a mixed approach," Aria suggested. "Court her and take her on dates like humans do, but make your interest known. Let her know she's the only one you're interested in."

That last part seemed obvious to me. How could I possibly be interested in anyone else?

"Is she latent?" Derric asked. "Or pure human?"

"I don't know," I admitted. "That's another can of worms. At some point, I have to tell her what I am."

It gnawed at me that I had already lied to her. Canada, eh? I just went along with her first guess about where I was from. And bodyguard for a super-important-not-quite-celebrity was the closest thing I could think of without outright saying I was part of a wolf pack.

"That's tough. You can't always tell right away."

Sawyer's voice was low, lazy. Like he was drunk or half-asleep. His eyes were half-closed, lulled into utter relaxation by his mate's head massage. Still, he kept a protective hand over Riley's belly. If anything triggered his wolf senses, he'd be alert and snarling at any perceived threat in the blink of an eye.

"The scent is the giveaway, I think," Fallon said. "Aria smelled like a human until I could scent her more closely."

"Mmm," Sawyer agreed. "It's subtle. You gotta get real close, nose right on her neck." He reached up, stroking affectionately along Riley's throat. "If she's one of us, you'll scent something underneath the human."

My heart started to pound, remembering how I did pick up something under Emmaline's scent as a wolf when she came near my cage.

"And since she's your mate, her scent will be something so delicious to you alone. It'll drive you crazy and be all you think about. You'll be dying for a taste." Fallon touched his drink to mine. "You're lucky you already know she's yours. It feels like you're losing your mind until you figure it out."

My gift of sight didn't feel like luck. Most of the time, it felt like a curse. The others had no idea how burdensome it was to see everyone's fate threads. It was private knowledge about people I had no right to know, but did anyway.

In some ways, I was glad my own thread appeared before me. I followed it straight to Emmaline. Well, straight into her car's front bumper, but that was neither here nor there. Most people would never know if there was another person destined for them, while all I had to do was follow a trail.

But on the other hand, I almost wished I didn't know. I could have met her organically somehow. Gotten to know her by being myself, without all this pressure of *fate* and *destiny* resting on my shoulders. Now that I knew, I felt paralyzed with indecision. I didn't want to screw up by saying or doing the wrong thing. She was my mate, my destined partner for life. I couldn't afford to be careless about this.

Fuck, I was usually the easy, carefree one, not riddled with anxiety about how to approach a female. I was supposed to give my packmates advice, not the other way around.

As if sensing my distress, Ruse knocked his shoulder into mine again. "Whatever you do, it'll be fine, Tryn. Fate has a way of working itself out."

I huffed out a laugh. When he wasn't being a dick, the Alpha's second could actually be a good friend sometimes. "By the moon, I hope you're right."

))))))●●●●(((((

Two hours later, I was in wolf form and crossing the invisible boundary between Shyftworld and the human world. I hadn't known this particular entrance existed until I followed my fate thread to Emmaline. This time, I was careful not to run across the country road leading into the human town where she lived.

My rear leg was still a bit stiff from the accident, and it would take another week or two for the muscles to fully regain strength. After a few miles of running though, I felt nearly good as new as I made my way toward the restaurant where Emmaline worked.

I'd stay far out of sight of any humans, of course. I just wanted to see her, or even pick up a fresh scent trail of hers. Just to make sure she was okay. If she hadn't called me because she was sick or something, I'd feel like an asshole for whining.

A breeze picked up and I paused in my run, lifting my nose to scent the air. Emmaline's fresh, lovely scent floated over me and I suppressed a growl of need. I still couldn't quite pick up the notes that made her unique, but Fallon wasn't wrong. I wanted to get close enough for a taste.

So she *was* working tonight, which meant she likely wasn't sick. Meaning she chose not to call me or had tried and couldn't get through.

A whine escaped my throat. My wolf was feeling insecure. He wanted her attention, her approval, and her hands in his fur. We'd just met this woman and as far as my animal was concerned, she had already rejected us. He couldn't understand it, not after she'd been so relieved that we'd chased off her creepy boss. We succeeded in protecting her. Did that not make us a worthy mate?

There was no reasoning with animal instincts. The best I could do was rein in my wolf, keep him under control while I pursued Emmaline the human way.

A door opened and my ears perked up, every muscle going still as a statue. Human voices, three of them, floated out into the still night air. Two female, one male. My wolf let out an excited huff at the sound of Emmaline's voice, our favorite sound in the world.

I crept through the trees and underbrush, staying out of sight of the humans as I followed the sound of their voices. Car doors opened and closed, then engines turned over. One set of footsteps continued to walk. Emmaline's. She and the others must have just finished work for the night.

Staying among the trees lining the street, I followed her home. She walked briskly and I kept a few paces behind, my nose and eyes steadily focused on her. To my relief, it was a short walk to her apartment. I hung back while she dug her keys out, careful not to step on a twig like the last time I saw her home.

Even though I didn't make a sound, Emmaline abruptly stopped trying to unlock her door and turned around.

Shit! I'm not here. You don't see me. If I kept saying that to myself, it would make it work, right?

It didn't work. She hit the flashlight on her phone and the bright beam immediately reflected my eyes.

"Fuck!" she exclaimed but didn't seem frightened. Instead, she extended her arm out toward me, moving the light out of my eyes. She squinted as if trying to see me more clearly. "Wolf? Is that you?"

I was so taken aback that she had sensed me there at all that I temporarily lost control of my wolf. He let out a soft bark of acknowledgment and started walking toward her.

No, don't! I stopped us short, keeping out of the apartment building's exterior lights, but then Emmaline closed the distance between us.

She came forward fearlessly, then stopped in a crouch a few feet away. "What are you doing here?" she asked. "You're not supposed to get this close to humans."

The only human I want to get close to is you.

My wolf wagged his tail and tapped his front paws on the ground. He wanted to get closer, to inhale her scent like a drug and to feel her fingers dig deeply into our fur. And moon be damned, I wanted that too. It was all I could do to keep my control because he kept fighting me, tugging at me like I had him on a literal leash.

"I'm glad to see you, even though you shouldn't be here," Emmaline admitted. "I hope this doesn't mean you've lost your pack."

My pack isn't complete until you're in it.

Emmaline's hand twitched at her side, almost like she was gathering the courage to hold it out to me.

No, not yet.

With a hard yank on my withering control, I forced my wolf to turn away and start running into the woods. I ran until her scent was just a memory instead of a tangible sensation in my nose.

Because if I let her touch me, I'd never be able to leave.

CHAPTER 8

EMMALINE

The next week, I functioned on autopilot and just went through the motions. Lynn, one of the owners of Buck's Peak, had no problem giving me extra hours, although it still wasn't quite a full-time schedule. Joey offered to train me as a bartender so I could help him at times, and I jumped at the chance.

When I wasn't working, I continued applying to vet residencies. At night, I sometimes looked out the window for my wolf, but he never came back after that first time.

I couldn't shake the sense that I was waiting for something, which was silly. Opportunities didn't fall into my lap. But some instinct, intuition, or whatever it was, told me not to leave Fulsburg yet, not until the right moment came.

So, I stayed and worked and continued dodging texts from my parents and my old coworkers at the clinic. The staff had been shocked at my sudden firing and demanded to know what had happened. I didn't completely ignore them, but I kept my answer vague.

Some had caught wind of the rumors about Dr. Stone's

confrontation with the big biker, but I neither confirmed nor denied it. Tryn wasn't from around here, he was just passing through and would likely never show up again. Dr. Stone was a powerful figure in the community and had much deeper pockets than mine. I absolutely didn't want to say anything that would make him come after me for slander or whatever. So I said nothing and waited for it all to blow over.

I'm just in a transition phase, I told myself. Like the space between chapters in a book. *The last era of my life has ended, and the new one hasn't begun yet.*

It was a slow weekday afternoon shift, just after the lunch rush, when I heard it.

The tables had been cleaned and I was hanging out with Joey, trying not to hover over the few customers with their coffees and newspapers, when a low, distant rumbling grew increasingly louder.

"Your knight in shining armor returns." Joey, who was taller than me, grinned as he looked out over the road leading up to the restaurant.

"What?" I didn't even deny what he said, stretching on my tiptoes, but I couldn't see over the parking lot. "Are you messing with me?"

"I'm a hundred percent serious. Did you ever call him?"

I lowered my heels to the floor and turned away from the window. "Um, no."

"Why the hell not? I thought you two were into each other?"

"I dunno," I mumbled, my face growing hot. "That was such a weird day."

I was certainly into Tryn but wasn't sure he felt the same. Sure, he gave me a number, but why make it a six-digit one? He wouldn't have forgotten to write his whole phone number down, would he? But if he wasn't interested, why would he come back?

We do serve good beer, and he is confident, I reasoned. *He's confident enough to not avoid a place entirely over...whatever giving a fake number means. Letting me down gently, maybe?*

I could see Tryn now, handling his motorcycle with masterful ease as he parked right in front of the restaurant. He wore a black leather vest over a white T-shirt this time. I caught a glimpse of the insignia on the back as he dismounted but couldn't quite make it out. Some kind of animal skull.

Before Tryn reached the front door, I scurried off to the sound of Joey's snickering. I shot him a dirty look over my shoulder but kept walking. He knew what I was doing— trying to look busy. Trying to look like I wasn't waiting for Tryn to show up.

He wasn't the *something* I was waiting for, despite every cell in my body lighting up with delight at his arrival. No, a tall, intimidating but disarmingly polite biker was not the start of the next chapter in my life. As fun as that was to fantasize, he couldn't be.

By the time I checked on my few customers and casually wandered back to the bar, Joey had already set Tryn up with a beer.

"There she is." Joey ended whatever small talk they were engaged in to stare pointedly at me.

I glared daggers at him in the split second before Tryn turned in my direction. "Hey, Emmaline. Nice to see you again."

The deep warmth of his voice betrayed nothing. His smile was polite, nothing more. He seemed a little guarded.

"Hey, Tryn. Right back at you." I leaned against the back of a barstool, unsure of what else to do.

"Working today, huh?" He took in my apron and work clothes.

"She gets off at four," Joey cut in before I could answer. With that, he headed for the back room, whistling loudly.

Now alone, Tryn and I both laughed nervously. "I'd kill him if he wasn't training me to bartend," I said, trying to diffuse some of the tension that permeated the air between us.

"He trying to be some kind of matchmaker?"

"It seems that way."

"Well, don't worry," Tryn said with an easy smile. "There's no hard feelings, and I can take a hint." He turned toward the bar like the conversation was over.

I stared at his handsome side profile for a moment. "What do you mean?"

He looked at me again, confusion knitting his brows together. "I mean, you never called me, so I figured..." He trailed off but lifted one shoulder in a shrug. "I'm not upset or anything. Just thought I'd shoot my shot, but like I said, no hard feelings."

I shook my head, even more confused as nervous laughter bubbled out of my mouth. "I thought you gave me a fake number."

Tryn's eyes narrowed. "Why would I do that?"

"I don't know, but the one you gave me is only six digits."

"Okay?"

He seemed genuinely confused as to what the issue was. The silence stretched on between us. Something wasn't adding up. How could he not know phone numbers were supposed to be seven digits?

Something seemed to dawn on him and he looked embarrassed, flushing a deep red. "Oh! Oh shit, I'm sorry. I forgot to tell you it's my personal cell. I've had that number for years. It's from back home, in Vargmore."

"And...that's why it has fewer numbers?" I asked, still confused.

He nodded. "Because it's such a small, independent community, our phone numbers have one less digit. I'm really sorry, I didn't even think about that." The smile he gave was wry. "Trust me, I would never give you a fake number."

"Oh." That was strange, but it did make more sense. "I guess I should have tried calling. I was...bummed when I thought it was fake."

Tryn's eyes lit up, his smile inching wider. "I was really hoping to hear from you," he admitted.

"Well, I'm glad you came back." I laughed. "Looks like the universe wanted us to have a do-over."

"Yeah." His voice grew lower, huskier. "I don't want to get you in trouble with another job though," he chuckled, looking past me.

I turned, following his gaze to the family of four that just walked in and stood by the hostess stand. And of course, the hostess had to call in sick last minute, which left seating up to the wait staff.

"Be right back," I told him, gathering up some menus for the new customers.

"Take your time, Emmaline." Tryn raised his beer to his lips. "I'm not going anywhere."

A slow trickle of customers came in over the next hour,

keeping me just busy enough that I couldn't talk to Tryn for any significant amount of time. *What the hell, universe,* I thought as I dropped off and picked up yet another drink order from Joey. *You giveth, then you keepeth busy.*

"So you're off in an hour?" Tryn asked when I came to the bar for another order.

I glanced at the clock. "Yes, thank God."

One corner of his mouth ticked up. "Do you want to have dinner with me?"

My pulse quickened, but I was somehow able to answer with cool confidence. "Well, yes, but there's a problem."

He frowned. "What's that?"

"This is the only decent restaurant in town, but to be honest, I'd rather not eat where I work."

"How about I put in a takeout order and we go for a ride?" Tryn nodded toward his bike. "I know a great place to watch the sunset. I'll tell Joey where it is so he can check in with you."

"That sounds great." And romantic. And it was really sweet that he was still being considerate of my safety. My insides swirled with sensations of fluttering and melting.

"What's your favorite thing here?" Tryn was already scanning a menu, one hand stroking his bearded jaw.

"You know what? Surprise me."

I didn't know where this confidence had come from, but I was high on it. This hot giant of a biker asked me on one date and I felt like I won the lottery. It was like there was another presence inside me, preening and pleased that he was finally seeing me, pursuing me.

That kind of confidence was so unlike me ,but for the moment, I was grateful it existed.

Tryn smiled wolfishly. "I do enjoy a challenge."

Joey placed the final drink on my tray and excitedly whispered, "Get it, girl," before I headed off to serve my table.

Naturally, the next hour crawled at a snail's pace. Despite that, I couldn't stop smiling. I felt like sunshine itself, no matter how much I tried to talk myself down. Sure, a date with a hot guy was great, but I still needed to find a vet residency as soon as possible. And depending how my applications panned out, I'd eventually have to leave Fulsburg, most likely for a larger city.

But those were tomorrow's problems. Four o'clock finally rolled around and I couldn't get my apron off fast enough. It was only when I checked the mirror in the break room that my confidence faltered.

I had barely any makeup on, and my work clothes had some grease stains on them. My hair wasn't having it. Honestly, the whole package wasn't having it. How could I go on a date looking like this?

He asked you out while you look like this, my out-of-nowhere confidence reminded me.

Even so, Tryn was giving me another chance after he thought I blew him off. He deserved a bit more effort from me.

He waited by the bar, chatting with Joey while holding a paper to-go bag and a brown, long-necked bottle with a swing-top cap. His eyes lit up, a smile pulling at his lips as I approached. "Hey. You ready?"

I played with my fingers, suddenly nervous. "Do you mind if we swing by my apartment so I can change? Can't say I was expecting to go on a date straight after work."

Tryn's eyes heated, his smile dropping. "You're perfect as you are," he practically growled. Then just as quickly, he added, "But yeah, of course. If you'd be more comfortable out of work clothes and," he paused with a small bite to his lip, "you're okay with me knowing where you live."

I felt no sense of alarm at that idea, no warning in my gut. Instead, I felt like I *wanted* him to see where I lived. Not that I would be inviting him inside right away, but I had this urge to see him in my space, among my things. I wanted him touching my things so they would smell like him...

"I'm okay with that," I said, shoving down those weird, overly-intimate thoughts. We had yet to go on *one* date for shit's sake.

"Cool." That stomach-flipping smile returned. "Shall we ride, then?"

"I've never been on a motorcycle before," I admitted as we left the restaurant. Even with his hands full, Tryn made sure to hold the door open for me.

"It's easy," he assured me. "You'll get the hang of it by the time we get to your place."

"How do you know I don't live in a distant cave up in the mountains?" I said it as a joke but saw what looked like momentary panic on Tryn's face before his features smoothed over.

"I've met a few cave trolls, and you don't quite fit the vibe," he joked back, securing the food and bottle in a compartment above his rear tire. "The engine gets loud, so you'll just have to shout directions into my ear and point where to go."

"I think I can handle that."

Tryn got on his motorcycle and started it up. The roar that came out of it made me wince at first, but it quickly calmed to a steady rumble.

"I got you, Emmaline." Tryn raised his voice to speak over the engine, but he sounded every bit as calm and gentle as when we sat next to each other at the bar. "You're completely safe." He held an arm out, which I used to steady myself as I climbed into the seat behind him. "I'll go slow through town, but hold onto me if you need to."

Forget need. How about if I want *to?* I smothered the thought as I settled on the bike, hyper aware of his closeness and our position. My legs were wide, inner thighs grazing the outsides of his. His back was like a wall in front of me, tall and broad in every direction. I didn't know what to do with my hands, so I decided on a light touch on his ribs.

"Okay," I said. "Head down this street and take a left at the stop sign."

As Tryn backed out of the parking lot and turned toward the direction I gave, a tingling, vibrating sensation took over my legs and hands.

And it wasn't just from the bike or the road.

CHAPTER 9

EMMALINE

We pulled up to my apartment only five minutes later, and I was loath to peel away from Tryn's warmth so soon.

"Grab a jacket, it'll get cold," he said when I hopped off the bike. "And don't worry about doing anything with your hair. The wind will blow it out."

I ran a hand through the mess on my head and let out a short laugh. "You mean it can get worse than this?"

"Quit that," he growled sternly, even though he was smiling. "You look great. Just dress warm and comfortable."

"Okay, be right back." I resisted the urge to skip up my walkway while he waited on the idling motorcycle. I was still nervous, but damn did it feel good to hear a man like *that* say I looked great.

I was in and out of my place within ten minutes, settling on dark wash jeans, a V-neck top that flattered my shape, and a quick brush through my hair. And, of course, a jacket. I would have loved to refresh my light makeup, but I didn't want to leave my biker man waiting *too* long.

"He's not mine," I reminded myself, stepping into my ankle boots right by the front door. "It's just one date."

Tryn was in the same spot when I stepped out and locked up, the bike rumbling gently under his massive thighs. Even though he was big and kind of intimidating, he seemed so steady, so calm. Like a boulder in the middle of a stream, everything just moved around him while he was still.

He unfolded his thicks arms, in no hurry when I approached, an appreciative smile forming on his lips as he gripped the handlebars. "All set?"

"Yeah." I resumed my seat behind him. "Let's ride."

"That's what I like to hear."

We accelerated forward, picking up speed as we drove onto one of the country roads leading out of town and through the wilderness. Tryn shifted a gear or something, and the bike seemed to jump forward, the sudden momentum pulling a gasp of fright from my chest.

Tryn immediately clasped a hand over mine that rested on his waist, his fingers tangling with mine for the briefest moment. "It's okay, I got you. We're going to speed up, so hang on and lean with me, okay?"

"Okay!" I tightened my grip and practically glued myself to the back of him like he was my safety net. Wherever he went, I would follow. Even if that meant careening over the edge of a cliff.

Nope, don't think about that. This is supposed to be fun.

And once I got over that initial jolt of fear, it was really, really fun.

The biggest risk I'd taken in life was going on a different educational and career path than what my parents wanted. I never took *actual* risks and had never been an adrenaline junkie. I'd never even gotten a speeding or parking ticket before.

I had never felt pure, physical exhilaration like this. The world passed by in a blur, wind whipping at my skin and clothes, all while I held onto a man who controlled the machine beneath us like it was an extension of his own body.

My parents would be appalled, and I reveled in knowing that.

We were maybe twenty minutes outside of town when the elevation got noticeably steep. The motorcycle growled loudly, vibrating with exertion as Tryn climbed a hill. Once we crested the peak, the bike quieted, and Tryn drove to a clearing carved out next to the road. There, he stopped and turned the motorcycle off.

"Oh, I love this lookout spot." Beyond the guardrail was a breathtaking view of one of the many valleys, covered in dense forest and sometimes capped with snow during the colder months.

"We're not quite there yet," Tryn said mysteriously. He slid from the bike and offered me a hand to help me off. "My secret spot is that way, just a short walk." He pointed to a barely marked trail I wouldn't have seen if he hadn't said anything.

"That's not suspicious for a first date at all."

Tryn looked a little sheepish as he took our food and drink from the compartments. "Go ahead and tell Joey you're here."

"Oh, right." I pulled out my phone and began typing out a text. "I'm surprised you remembered that and I forgot."

"I just want you to know that you can trust me," he said so softly I almost didn't hear.

I do, I wanted to say, but for some reason it felt like too much to say out loud. But I did trust Tryn, even though I barely knew him. Some men just gave women a bad gut feeling, even if they technically didn't act creepy or suspicious.

With Tryn, my gut feeling was the exact opposite. I felt an immediate sense of safety with him. He was being considerate and cautious, almost overly so, when he didn't need to be. I would still feel safe even if he didn't suggest I check in with a friend while out in the woods with him. Honestly, I found his caution endearing.

But what if my gut was wrong and I was just being naive? I had never suspected Dr. Stone of being a creep.

I wasn't exactly a virgin, but I was still woefully inexperienced with men, so there was definitely some naivety at play. Despite that, Tryn seemed to have come from a completely different world. He wanted me to feel safe, and that alone put him above all other men I'd known. Well, except Joey, who wasn't even interested in women.

"Would you carry the blanket and cups?" Tryn nodded at the open compartment on his bike.

I looked inside and pulled out a folded picnic blanket and short stack of red Solo cups. "So you were planning this, huh?"

His smile was warm and heartfelt. "I try to always be prepared, especially when it comes to sunset picnic dates with pretty veterinarians."

I laughed, hugging the blanket to my chest. "You go on a lot of those?"

"I'm one for one so far. Shall we?"

I followed him to the start of the trail and then into the dense wooded area. The trees were really close together here, like they grew completely wild and hadn't been thinned out by the fire service in decades, if ever.

Tryn kept his long-legged pace slow so I never lost track of him. I squeezed the blanket as I walked, even putting my face to it and exhaling to warm my cheeks and nose. The tree cover blocked out most of the sunlight and the late afternoon air was chillier here.

Keeping the blanket close to my face, I inhaled and then...*oh wow*.

My nose pulled in the scent of fresh leather and bright green moss. Those two scents mixed together in a chemical cocktail that was like crack to my brain. I wanted to wrap this blanket around my shoulders and become enveloped in this scent. Something about it conveyed warmth, contentment, and safety. Screw the blanket actually, I wanted to bottle this up and bathe in it.

"Almost there. Not much farther," Tryn informed me.

It's his scent, I realized with an odd mix of giddiness and shame. It was a major plus that he smelled so damn good, but now I felt like a weirdo for being so entranced by it.

"You good, Emmaline?" He paused and turned back to check on me.

I lifted my face away from the blanket just before he saw. "Yeah, perfect."

"Great." He resumed walking the trail. "It's just through here."

We walked in silence for another hundred or so yards. Tryn made sure to hold low-hanging branches out of my way while I huffed his picnic blanket as discreetly as I could.

Suddenly, it felt like invisible threads dragged over my

skin and hair. I saw nothing, but they felt soft, wispy and fragile like spiderwebs.

"Oh, fuck!" I dropped the blanket and cups as realization hit me and started frantically batting at my own face and hair.

"Emmaline?" I heard the concern in Tryn's voice but couldn't see him through my squeezed-shut eyelids.

"I just walked into a spiderweb!" How the web missed him and hit me square in the face, I had no clue, but now my skin was crawling from head to toe. "Is it still on me? Oh fuck, get it off!"

"Come here." Callused fingers took hold of my hand and gently pulled me forward. Immediately, the webbing sensation was gone. "I think you got it all."

I peeked one eye open, and then the other. Tryn was still holding my hand, trying to hide the amusement in his face. "Are you sure it's all gone?"

He nodded and leaned over to inspect the top of my head, struggling to make his expression serious. "Yup, not a web to be seen."

I checked myself over once more, then turned back to look at the way I came. "Stealthy fuckers. I never saw a thing."

"I take it spiders are the one animal you don't like?" he mused.

"That's a nice way of putting it. I actually like that they eat flies and other bugs, I've just never liked the feel of their webs on me—oh, shit." I picked up the blanket and cups I dropped, running my hand over it to scrape off the dead leaves and dirt. "I'm sorry, I messed this up when I freaked out."

"It's supposed to get dirty." Tryn chuckled. "We'll just put that side down for our picnic. Look, we're here."

We had emerged from the woods to a rocky ridge overlooking more forested mountains, as well as a grassy meadow and a small lake that reflected the mountains like glass.

"Oh wow, I had no idea this was here!" Nearby, there was a slope down to the meadow and lake that looked gentle and not a far walk. I almost wanted to picnic near the water instead of back here. "What lake is that? I must have missed seeing it on the local maps."

"I'm not sure of its name." Tryn set his things down and gently took the blanket from me to spread it on the ground. "It might be too small for any maps. But it's pretty, isn't it?"

"It's gorgeous." The late afternoon sun cast long shadows and made the water shimmer. The moon, just past half full, shone high in the sky while its counterpart, the sun, began its descent.

When I turned away from the scene, Tryn was already sitting on the blanket, pouring beer from the swingtop bottle into the red cups and smiling at me. My whole body heated, wondering if he'd been looking at me the whole time I was staring at the lake.

"Thirsty?" He held out one of the cups to me.

Man, you have no idea. "Thanks." I accepted the drink and sat next to him on the blanket, sighing at the beautiful scene. "How did you find this place?"

"Just exploring." He pulled our food containers from the bag and held one out to me with a grin. "Did I guess your favorite right?"

I opened the styrofoam lid and couldn't hold back the laugh that burst out of me. "Did Joey tell you?"

"No, I swear." He held up his hands. "You just seemed like a steak sandwich girl, so that's what I went for."

"Buck definitely makes the best tri-tip sandwich in all of California. What did you get?"

"Fish and chips. Joey's recommendation."

"Also a good choice."

"Cheers." He touched his red plastic cup to mine. "Thanks for coming out with me, Emmaline."

"Thanks for inviting me." I swallowed a bite of my sandwich and added, "You can call me Emmy if you like."

Tryn cocked his head as if thinking about it. "I like Emmaline, actually. It sounds musical."

I hid my big, goofy grin behind a sip of beer. "Aw, thank you."

"It's way better than my name, which sounds like something stuck in your throat."

"That is not true!" I laughed. "Although your name is really unique. Does it mean something?"

Tryn nodded. "It means bear in an ancient language almost no one speaks anymore."

"Oh, like an indigenous language?"

"Something like that."

"And why were you named bear?"

"Because I was born huge and hairy as fuck." He grinned at my laughter. "Much as I am now."

"You mean you came out of the womb looking like this?" I waved my hand over him.

"Pretty much, yeah."

"No way, I bet you were a cute baby."

He shrugged. "In the same way bears are cute, I guess."

"Bears are very cute! I bottle fed a cub at work a little

while ago and it made my whole week. They have extremely sharp claws and teeth, though."

Trynn finished chewing his food and smirked. "What's better, bears or wolves?"

There was no question in my mind, but I pretended to think anyway. "It's gotta be wolves." I playfully nudged him with my elbow. "Sorry, bear."

"That's alright," he said with a mock disappointed sigh.

"You're my favorite bear, if it's any consolation." My pulse quickened. Shit, was that coming on too strong? The beer seemed to have loosened my tongue already. Or was I just *that* comfortable around Tryn?

"And you're my favorite vet," he answered with that slow smile. In a blink, his expression turned serious. "But you're implying that you also have a favorite wolf. Should I be jealous?"

"Ah, you got me," I admitted with a giggle.

"I'm hurt. Who is it?" Tryn frowned but amusement lit up his eyes.

"The wolf I told you about the first time we talked, remember?"

"Oh, the one you released?" His voice went soft.

"Yeah. I don't know, there was something special about him. Like I knew releasing him was the right thing to do, but it still hurt to let him go. And he acted differently when I was around, it was so strange. Like he could flip the switch from wild animal in captivity to a friendly dog wanting to be petted."

I shook my head, laughing sheepishly at Tryn's intense look. "Sorry, don't get me started on animal behavior, it's a whole thing with me."

"He probably knew that you wanted to help," Tryn said. "That you were different from the others."

"It's possible he might have picked up something in my scent that calmed him. I don't know what else could set me apart though. I'm just another over-educated mid-twenties girl trying to find a job." I cringed inwardly, not meaning to go the self-deprecating route.

"You will," Tryn said easily, like it was a simple fact. "The wolf didn't know your job struggles, but something about you, Emmaline, touched him where others couldn't. That's got nothing to do with your occupation and everything to do with who you are as a person."

The sun was getting lower in the horizon, bringing a biting chill to the air. "You have a lot of confidence in someone you barely know," I said, tucking my arms close to my body.

"I told you I have a good sense about people." He set aside his food container and cup, scooting an inch closer to me on the blanket. "Cold?"

"Just a little." I rubbed my palms together, then found both hands enveloped in his much larger ones.

It was all I could do to suppress a moan as he rubbed my fingers gently. He felt like I'd stuck my hands in a preheating oven.

"How are you so warm?" I found myself scooting closer to him until the sides of our hips touched.

"I always run hot." He continued rubbing and massaging into my knuckles. "It's a bear thing."

I laughed. "Sadly, I am merely human."

"Somehow I doubt that," he murmured.

The light turned golden and then orange as we inched closer together. Tryn slid one arm behind me, rubbing warmth into my back as the sun became obscured by the distant trees. The temperature dropped even further, and I found myself nestled against his side, seeking his body heat while my head rested on his shoulder.

I got more of that fresh leather and moss in my nose and sighed with contentment, relaxing into the big, gentle man at my side. Tryn massaged my upper back, teasing the ends of my hair as he caressed the base of my neck. His head turned, and I felt the rasp of his stubble against my cheek and temple.

"Emmaline," he whispered, lips moving against my eyebrow.

My pulse spiked as I felt his lips trail lower, tracing the length of my nose. All I had to do was look up and I'd be kissing him.

And I *wanted* to kiss him. What better way to end the best date I'd ever been on? My eyelids fell shut and my lips parted as I lifted my face.

But my mouth did not meet Tryn's.

"Emmaline, look," he whispered.

My eyes opened. He was looking straight ahead now, not at me.

I followed his gaze and the length of his arm pointing to the meadow and lake in the valley below. They were barely visible at this distance in the fading light, but I saw several shapes moving.

"Oh my God, are those wolves?" I whispered in awe.

Tryn nodded. "It's a whole pack."

One wolf threw its head back, letting out a long howl. Others quickly joined in, creating a chorus of voices in a single song. It was the most haunting, beautiful sound I'd ever heard. I'd heard wolves howl before but never a whole pack like this. This was an incredibly rare moment for humans to see, and I wondered if Tryn knew that.

"Did you know they would be here?" I asked him as the howls faded.

"Had a lucky guess." He gave me a wry grin. "I've seen them wander through here before. Didn't think they'd start howling, though."

After singing their song and drinking from the lake, the pack moved on, disappearing through the trees, and the sun finally slipped below the horizon. For a brief moment, I wondered if my wolf from the clinic was part of that pack. If he'd been down there, wild and howling in the place he belonged.

"That was incredible." My attention returned to Tryn's lips and how close they were. "Thank you for bringing me here."

"My pleasure." His face turned toward mine again, his breath blowing gentle warmth over my lips and nose. "I owe them a round of beer."

"Who?" I giggled. "The wolves?"

"Yeah. You know how hard it is to convince a pack of wild animals to do their thing while I'm trying to impress a girl?"

I laughed, the motion drawing me closer to him, practically nuzzling his neck. "Seriously, don't give beer to wolves."

"If you say so, Doc."

Tryn's warm hand came to my cheek. He traced my jaw, gently tilting my face upwards. The next thing I felt was the soft, pressing heat of his lips on mine. My mouth parted in surprise—I thought the moment for a kiss had passed—and he slid into the opening, capturing me in a kiss that was warm, sweet, but unmistakably heated and sensual.

He made it brief but only barely pulled away, lips still grazing mine while my breath shook. "This good, Emmaline?"

"Yes."

I had barely finished breathing out the word when he kissed me again. It wasn't a surprise this time, but something surged in my body that I had no control over. Desire like I'd never felt before flooded my veins, turning me to fiery liquid. My tongue stroked against Tryn's, devouring him as much as he was me, my arms going around his broad shoulders.

Buried under the heady desire, under the taste of him, his firm hold on my waist, and his soft growls as he plundered my mouth, a tiny voice yelled that this wasn't me. I was inexperienced and awkward with men on a good day. No one pictured me when they thought of the type of woman who made out with a biker on a first date. My parents would be utterly ashamed.

But I didn't care. All I wanted was to slide my legs apart so Tryn could move between them. I wanted his clothes gone so I could feel the heat of his skin. I wanted *my* clothes gone so he could show me what those big hands were capable of. I wanted his teeth in me, marking me. *Oh, fuck yes.* I needed his teeth marks in my skin to match the ones I would give him...

Wait, what the fuck?

I froze, my whole body going rigid to the point where Tryn immediately noticed.

He pulled back, frowning as cold air rushed into the spaces where his touch had warmed me. "You okay?"

"Yeah...yes, I'm fine." I felt dazed, a little breathless from his kisses, and extremely confused as to where those thoughts had come from. Biting and teeth marks? What the hell?

"You don't look so sure." Tryn moved further away, and the distance he put between us was colder than the chilly evening air. "I should probably take you home anyway."

"Oh. Okay."

As we cleaned up our picnic, a scandalous thought arose. One that was very much unlike me, just like those thoughts of biting and marking.

When he takes you home, invite him inside. To your bed.

On a first date? No way, I barely know him!

You trust him. You like how he touches you. Why not? You're a big girl, be a little wild.

It felt like arguing with two sides of myself, which never happened before. I had never felt so conflicted about something, like there were two of me sharing one body. Before meeting Tryn, I never even would have entertained the thought of bringing a man home and sleeping with him after a first date.

But Tryn wasn't like any other man I'd met. If he accepted what I offered, I knew it would be an incredible night. But was that all I wanted? Or could there be something more here?

The whole date, from the motorcycle ride to the kiss, had been thoughtful and sweet. Would he have done all this if he just wanted to get in my pants?

"Ready to go, Emmaline?" Tryn tapped the flashlight on his phone, lighting the way to the trail back to the lookout spot.

I folded the picnic blanket over my forearm. "Ready when you are."

"I'll watch for those spiderwebs." He chuckled.

I followed after him, my nose to the blanket as if to draw courage from his scent.

When he pulls up to your place, ask him to come inside. Just ask him!

The entire ride home, my conflicted feelings never went away. I didn't know who this other side of me was.

And I wasn't sure if I liked it.

CHAPTER 10

TRYN

I dropped Emmaline off at home with a goodnight and a chaste kiss. If I had even an inkling of taking things further, I'd be in huge fucking trouble.

I rode home while rock hard with her sweet taste lingering in my mouth. Blackberries. That was her scent and the flavor that greeted my tongue when her lips parted for me. And fucking moon above, I loved blackberries.

My wolf was ravenous for her. After kissing her on the blanket, he was more than ready to bite her. To leave a mark and claim her, making her permanently off limits to all others.

If Emmaline was from Vargmore, it would be a quick conversation. *Do you want my bite? Would you like to claim me too?* If she felt positively, we'd proceed with the marking and most likely, fuck right then and there under the sky. She would be mine and I would be hers. Simple. Instinctual.

But of course it couldn't be that easy. Fate had paired me with someone who believed my kind were fictional monsters. I had to be careful around my human, and that became especially clear when she froze up on me mid-kiss. Instincts couldn't be relied upon, not fully. I had to use my rational, human side for this.

The next day, I decided to pay my grandmother a visit. After my werewolf grandfather died in the war with the vampires almost a century ago, she moved into the elder witch's lodge. I took the scenic route, riding through Vargmore with the fresh mountain air whipping over me.

Humans were generally more individualistic than werewolves and didn't have the same need for a pack as we did. They were content enough to live alone or just with their mates or single family units. The elder humans and witches however, often lived together to help support each other. Those who had lived in Vargmore for generations alongside us wolves tended to be more community-oriented. It wasn't quite a pack but close enough.

Gran sat outside on the lodge's wraparound porch with another elderly witch, Griselda, who owned The Manticore's Cauldron, a witchcraft supply shop and apothecary. The two of them were talking over tea when I pulled up. A huge smile took over Gran's face when she saw me, and she started to move the blanket from her lap.

"No, don't get up," I told her when I cut the engine, hurrying up the front steps to her.

"Oh shut it, pup. Movement keeps me young." She stood despite my protests, holding her arms wide. "How are you, son?"

"Good. I didn't mean to interrupt." I hugged her as tightly as I dared, leaning down to plant a kiss on top of her head. I visited Gran once a week at minimum, but she always greeted me like we'd spent months apart.

"Silly bear, you're not interrupting a thing. Sit down."

She resumed her seat, putting the blanket over her lap. "Selda was just telling me she saw Riley and Sawyer in the Cauldron this morning."

"Cleared out my peppermint supply," the other witch chuckled as I took the seat across from them. "I guess the morning sickness has started. Poor thing."

Gran folded her hands in her lap and nodded. "Mm-hm, it's no easy thing to birth a werewolf pup, but she'll get through it. We all did."

"Thank the moon I didn't." Griselda laughed. "Birthing humans is hard enough. I don't envy you wolves at all."

I looked at Gran. "Did you know Dad was going to be a wolf?" I had never thought about it before but found myself wondering about the probabilities. Technically, I was three-quarters werewolf, one quarter human. In the far off future, if Emmaline and I were to work out and start our own family, were we more likely to have wolf or human offspring? Especially if she was fully human herself.

"I knew because the moon showed me," Gran said solemnly. "I saw visions of him fully grown when he was still in my belly. Running on all fours, howling, hunting. A strong, beautiful beast." She went quiet for a few moments. The same conflict with the vampires that took my grandfather, her mate, also took my parents. Sawyer's too. At least half of the wolves in our pack were orphans because of that war.

"But if you were wondering about the statistics," Gran continued, her keen eyes trained on me, "it's a fifty-fifty chance. The offspring of a human-werewolf pairing is equally likely to take on the abilities of either parent." She lifted a teacup to her lips, hawk eyes still on me. "But that's not really what you're asking, is it, bear?"

I smiled, knowing she would see right through me. "I'm actually wondering how you can tell if a human is a latent werewolf."

"Oh!" Griselda leaned forward with interest. "Have you found someone, Tryn?"

"He's found his mate," Gran said affectionately. "Your fate thread is shimmering, bear. It looks strong and healthy."

"Yeah, we've met and are...getting to know each other. It's going well, I think. She's brilliant, driven, and so kind, selfless."

Gran's lips quirked. "But she's human? Or least human-presenting?"

"Not only that but deeply entrenched in the human world." I sighed. "She grew up there, it's all she knows. She has no idea about us, and I don't know how to broach it. I've already lied to her about so much, and I feel terrible about it. I want her to know who I really am, but...it could backfire badly if I'm not careful."

"What makes you think she's a latent wolf?" Griselda took a noisy sip of tea.

"She doesn't have just a human scent. She smells like blackberries when I'm close enough to pick it up. She also loves wolves."

"Aw, what a dear," Gran cooed.

"She's a veterinarian."

"Ooh, a doctor!" Griselda playfully slapped Gran's fore-arm. "Lucky you, Midge. A fancy doctor for a grand-daughter."

I smiled down at the table. If Emmaline were here, she'd balk at being called a doctor. She'd insist she was just an intern, not even a resident yet. But if things worked out, she'd find people here who were impressed by her, who would never tear down her accomplishments.

"Well, those are certainly positive signs," Gran hedged, ever the realist. "But the truth is, we don't have much information on latent wolves. Fallon and Sawyer's mates are the first we've truly seen in centuries, maybe even a millennium. Most of the wolves who escaped to the human world never came back here. Until recently, the theories about latent wolves were just part of our folklore."

"From talking to Aria and Riley, it seems their wolves began awakening from dormancy once they began spending time with their mates," Griselda said. "They started feeling like another being was inside them, talking to them. And when things became *physical,*" she arched an eyebrow at me, "more of those possessive mating instincts came through. The urge to bite and claim, and to have animalistic sex with their mate as soon as possible. Both women told me this, so there does appear to be a pattern of symptoms."

"That's good to know, but two people is hardly a sample size," Gran pointed out.

"I know, but it's a promising start."

I scratched my beard, contemplating. "I could ask her about the biting, maybe. She seems a little shy, though. And things are still new between us."

"She'll be less shy once her wolf starts making demands." Gran chuckled, then became stern. "Be careful, bear. You shouldn't be out in the human world near or on the full moon."

"I know, Gran."

"Yes, you *know,* but the pull to your mate will be extraordinarily strong during that time, especially if you have not yet claimed her. It may be physically painful to stay away, but until she knows what's going on, you *have* to."

"Right. I got it."

"She will likely feel the effects too, if her wolf is indeed waking up."

The thought of Emmaline alone and unbearably horny on the full moon was enough to make my wolf whine in distress. *I know, buddy,* I told him. It was awful to think of our mate in such pressing need, so much frustration that only I could satisfy, and being forced to stay away from her. It would feel like torture for her, and certainly would be for me, knowing I couldn't be there to soothe those aches and pains.

"The full moon is in a week, by the way," Gran said.

My teeth clenched in my jaw. "I know that, Gran."

The ancient witch held up a finger in warning. "Don't you growl at me, pup. I'm not one of your packmates you can snarl and bark at."

"I'm sorry."

I forced myself to relax. Gran was so much more than a witch, more than my family. She was a pillar of Vargmore, descended from one of the first witch families to make their home in the land of the wolves. The moon's magic ran deeply through her bloodline. She was ancient and wise, commanding respect even from the oldest, most grizzled wolves in the territory.

Gran softened at my apology. "Don't try to rush things, bear. Ensure your human feels safe with you. This will be a hard moon to get through, but you will get through it. And so will she."

I nodded. "Thank you, Gran."

She smiled broadly at me. "Trust in fate, son. Trust that she will love and accept you for exactly who you are."

"I hope so." Pushing my chair back, I proceeded to stand, and my grandmother did the same. "No, don't get up—"

My protests were met with a growl that would make any wolf lower their head, and a loving hug wrapped around my waist. The moment we separated, my phone went off.

"Is that her?" Griselda's eyes widened eagerly.

"No, it's Derric." I too had hoped it was Emmaline, giving my apparently strange six-digit number a try.

"Tell the Alpha I said hello." Gran settled back in her chair with her blanket and her tea.

"Will do." I bent to kiss her forehead before answering the phone on the way back to my bike. "Hey, Alpha."

"Where are you?" Derric's voice was clipped, all business.

"Witch's lodge. I was just visiting Gran. She says hello, by the way."

"Meet us at the northern border by Helios." He didn't even acknowledge Gran, which meant this was super serious.

"What's going on?"

"Vampire sightings in the angels' city."

Well, that was some bad fucking news. "I'm on my way." I ended the call and rode like hell toward Helios City.

))))) ◗ ● ◖ (((((

THE ALLEGED VAMPIRE sightings ended up being a huge waste of time. We couldn't smell the blood suckers anywhere near where they supposedly had been, according to a few very unreliable witnesses. When we interviewed more people in the area, both angel and human, no one had seen any vampires. Derric and the leader of the angels, Camael, got into a shouting match which had to be broken up before it turned into a physical fight. That was our cue to turn tail and leave the winged assholes to deal with their own problems.

Our relationship with the angels was...complicated. Technically, we were allies. They had joined our side in the war against the vampires. Derric and Camael got along well most of the time. But it was times like these, when they called us for aid, that really showed the friction between our two species.

Angels were fucking snobs by nature, quite frankly. Maybe it was the flying thing, or all the folklore about them being divine beings or whatever, but they seemed to think of all other species as beneath them. Especially vampires, who spent most of their time underground to escape the sun, but despite our alliance, I got a sense that werewolves weren't considered much higher on the totem pole.

We were creatures of the earth, ruled by our senses, instincts, and the moon. Sure, we acted like animals, because *we fucking were*. And the angels, looking down at us from the skyline of their pristine city, their wings shimmering in the sun, didn't see us as equals. It was never explicitly stated but more of a general feeling my pack-mates and I got whenever we interacted with them. Sawyer often grumbled that they treated us like guard dogs, commanding us to bark and growl at every tiny perceived threat while they flew well out of range of any danger.

After a bullshit call like this, I couldn't agree more.

I was annoyed that most of my day had been wasted. Almost all of the pack went to Stout & Spirit to unwind with some drinks, but I didn't feel like getting rowdy with them tonight. I wanted quiet, peace. Thank the moon the pack lodge was empty.

I showered and settled into bed just as my phone rang. "Unknown Caller" flashed across my screen and I answered it with a puzzled, "Hello?"

Light static crackled across the line, but my mate's voice was clear. "Hi, Tryn? It's Emmaline."

"Hey." The word became long and drawn out with the smile spreading across my face. "Finally gave it a shot, huh?"

"Yeah." She laughed. "I'm surprised it worked. Took a minute to connect, though."

"I'm glad you called." I brought one arm behind my head, relaxing into the mattress at the sound of her voice. Closing my eyes, I imagined she was here, talking to me in person with her head on my chest. "How are you?"

"Good." There was a pause, and then she breathed out a heavy sigh. "I'm exhausted, actually. It's been a long day."

"Yeah? Tell me about it." I shifted in bed, sitting up a little higher. "Busy day at the restaurant?"

"Crazy busy. I worked the lunch and dinner shift, and we were packed the whole time. I also didn't sleep great, so you know, compounding exhaustion."

"Sorry to hear that. Any reason why you didn't sleep well?" I wondered if the approaching full moon was already affecting her. The lack of a mating bite and impending sexual frustration was a hell of a sleep killer, or so I'd heard.

"I don't really know. My brain was just wired after you dropped me off, so I stayed up applying for more jobs."

"How's the job search going?"

"It's going," she sighed. "Nothing noteworthy yet. Anyway, I'm sorry to complain. How was your day?"

"Don't be sorry. You can unload on me anytime." Fuck, I really wished she was here in person and not a disembodied voice in my ear. "My day was fine. I visited my grandmother in the morning, then just dealt with work stuff the rest of the day."

"Oh, are you close with your grandmother?" Emmaline's voice pitched a little higher.

"Yeah, she's the one that raised me, as well as one of my close friends that works with me."

"I want to say that's really sweet, but I guess it's also sad because it means something happened with your parents."

"They died a long time ago. My friend's parents too. There was a…a conflict when we were younger. It affected a lot of families in our community."

"Oh, Tryn. I'm so sorry, that's awful."

The earnest sympathy in her voice was a shock to my system, and I realized she was the first person outside of Vargmore that I'd told about my parents' deaths. Not that the other survivors of the vampire war weren't sympathetic. It was just different because we all had been in it. My losses were everyone's in Vargmore. We all grieved together, leaned on each other, but we also hyper focused on survival. Many thought that the war would cause our extinction.

After the truce was signed and the borders between our territories established, we were all focused on rebuilding. The Howling Death pack was formed, and then we became a motorcycle club. In all that time, I couldn't think of a single instance in which anyone took the time to truly mourn and reflect on how devastating our losses were.

And it wasn't just the deaths that devastated but also all the families that fled to the human world and suppressed their abilities. My parents and grandparents' generations believed those wolves were lost forever. Now, with the emerging latent wolves, I felt a sweet spark of hope emerge. Our people were finding their kind and coming home.

"Thank you for saying that," I said to Emmaline after a long pause. "I don't often think about how awful it was."

"I can understand why; it must be so painful."

Animals were good at hiding their pain. And werewolves were no different.

"I'm lucky to still have Gran." The old crone was probably going to outlive me, but Emmaline didn't need the specifics of that. "And I have my friends, my pa—uh, my community. So I never went through it alone."

"I'm glad you had that." Her voice became wistful. "It sounds nice, to never have to go through something alone."

"Eh, the guys can be overbearing sometimes. But yeah, it does help when you need someone to just be there."

Emmaline went quiet, and my wolf howled mournfully inside my skull. My chest ached with the thought of how alone she must feel. She moved to that small town in the middle of nowhere for a dream career that discarded her. She didn't talk much about her family or close friends. And while she seemed on good terms with her coworkers at the restaurant, they seemed more like acquaintances than true friends.

Fucking moon, I was dying to leap out of bed and drag her back home with me. She didn't know it yet, but she never needed to be alone again.

"Are you off tomorrow?" I asked, hoping and praying for a certain answer.

"Yes, thank God." She sighed while I pumped my fist through the air. "My one full day off this week. I'm going to sleep in until noon."

"I fully support that. Sounds like you need the rest."

She remained quiet, as if waiting for me to ask what was on my mind.

"After you're well-rested," I said, my heartbeat picking up speed, "any chance I could see you tomorrow?"

"I would love that." I could hear the smile in her voice, but then she hesitated. "But aren't you in Canada?"

"Canada?" I repeated with a laugh.

"I assumed you were back home since you mentioned seeing your grandmother. Unless I misunderstood and she lives close by?"

"Oh, right! Right." I rubbed my brow and once again felt the pang of regret for lying to her. "No, she's actually pretty close by. I'm still in your neck of the woods."

"Oh, good."

The relief in her voice made me grin with contentment. "What time should I pick you up?"

"How about six? That should give me enough time to properly veg out or run any errands I need to do."

"Sounds perfect," I murmured into the phone. Then before I could think too much about it, "I can't wait to see you."

"Can't wait to see you too…" She sounded sleepy, like she was already drifting off.

"Get a good ten hours for me. I'll be there before you know it."

"Mm-hmm. Goodnight, Tryn…"

She was already halfway gone, if not more. And I found it so sweet and endearing that I found it physically painful to *not* be holding her against my chest as she drifted off.

"Goodnight, Emmaline."

I stayed on the phone until she was breathing deeply in my ear. When I ended the call and the silence of my bedroom poured into my awareness like a can of black paint, I knew.

Human or latent werewolf, it didn't matter.

I was a goner for this woman.

CHAPTER 11
EMMALINE

Tryn appeared on my doorstep at five minutes to six, looking like sex on a stick in his usual leather vest, white T-shirt, faded jeans, and biker boots. He also carried a small bundle of wildflowers held together by a length of twine.

"Please don't tell me you're allergic," he said at my open-mouthed shock. "If you are, I'm really sorry. I just thought—"

"No! No, I'm not allergic." Right then I noticed his panicked expression and laughed. "No one's ever brought me flowers before, that's all. Come in, and thank you. They're beautiful."

He stepped across the threshold and closed the door behind him, taking up a massive amount of space in my one-bedroom apartment. "I wondered if flowers would be a risky move," he admitted sheepishly.

"Not at all, it's really sweet of you." I took the bundle from him and raised up to my tiptoes, lifting my face to his.

Tryn met me halfway, leaning down with a half-smile

to give me a kiss that was warm, sensual, and lingering. The desire I'd felt on our first date roared back to life with a vengeance. Earlier today, we'd made plans to visit a brewery in the next town over, but all I really wanted to do was climb him like a tree and show him to the bedroom.

"I'll put these in water," I whispered as the kiss ended, amazed that I didn't say, *You're making me wetter than water.*

"I'm glad you like them," he murmured, straightening to his full height. While I looked for something that would make a passable vase, Tryn's gaze swept over my apartment. "You've got a nice place."

"Oh, please." I laughed, filling up a mason jar in the sink. "It's basically a dorm room. You don't have to be polite."

"No, I mean it." He took a few steps into my living area, head nearly brushing the ceiling as he stood in front of my bookshelves. "It's cozy in here, like a den. Feels like you."

"Well, thanks." I didn't entirely know what he meant, but it felt like a compliment. My chest warmed at the words. "What's your place like?"

"Not too different," he answered easily, before I could wonder if that question was too invasive. "Small, near the woods. I live with a bunch of guys all around me so yeah, a lot like a dorm room."

"Oh really? Is that just when you're working or when you go back home too?"

Tryn's jaw seemed to tense up for a moment, but then it passed. His easy smile returned. "I'm pretty much always working, so yeah."

It was a vague answer, one that seemed to dodge the question. I tried not to feel bothered by it, remembering that he couldn't tell me everything about his job yet. He was secretive about some things because he had to be, not because he was hiding a criminal background or a wife. There was no way I'd feel so attracted to someone who was intentionally deceiving me.

Right?

"Ready to go?" He went back to standing by the doorway.

"Yeah. Just let me put my coat and shoes on." I stepped into a pair of ankle boots and bent over to zip them up. They weren't biker-like in the slightest but were cute enough. It wasn't until after I opened the coat closet, grabbed one, and put my arms through the sleeves that I realized that Tryn had been staring at me the whole time. "What?" I looked down, wondering if I'd spilled water or anything else.

"Nothing," he said softly. "You're just beautiful, that's all."

The simple, earnest compliment stunned me. Men that looked like him didn't find women like me beautiful. I'd been teased about being nerdy, bookish, always studying instead of partying and having fun. Never beautiful.

And I had a feeling Tryn knew that as he reached for one of my hands, gently pulling me toward the door. "You deserve to hear that every day." He leaned down and kissed me, which I was grateful for, because I still didn't have words to speak with. We parted only after I started to feel breathless. I was beginning to realize Tryn didn't do short kisses. "Now let's ride and taste some beer." He smiled against my lips.

I was already drunk on his taste, his wild mossy scent, his voice, and the ridiculous, crazy idea that he might actually like me, but I nodded and found my voice again. "Yeah, let's go."

)))))❭❭●❬❬((((

OUR DATE at the brewery was honestly a blur. I knew with some distant awareness that we sampled beers and ate tacos from an excellent local food truck. But the focus of all my senses seemed to home in on Tryn. He warmed my freezing cold hands like on our first date, since most of the brewery seating was outside. We talked and laughed the whole evening, but it was the physical connection I craved like a starving woman. Every kiss on the cheek, roughened by his stubble, nearly left me gasping. Every embrace of those thick arms pressing me to his broad chest had my hands itching to dive under his clothes to feel the heat of his bare skin.

I tried to be in the moment, to listen earnestly to the stories he told about playing pranks with his best friend as a youngster, but this feverish need consumed me. My thoughts turned to kissing more intimate places, of bare skin gliding on skin. Of hardness and softness, instinct and touch.

On our first date, the intensity of these sexual thoughts were unnerving to the point of making me uncomfortable. Now, I was just tired of fighting them. Tryn was the only person I'd ever met who made me feel this way, who made me realize how starved for an intimate connection I really was.

At long last, the brewery gave their last call and Tryn

settled up our tab. He wouldn't let me pay and playfully restrained my hands so that I couldn't reach my wallet. It only made me imagine him pinning my hands down while thrusting into me.

His large hand rested on my leg on our drive home, the other confidently steering the motorcycle. My body was a furnace in the chilly mountain air, nerves alight with sensation while he gently massaged my thigh and traced soothing circles on my knee. Emboldened by my desire— and maybe the beers—my hands found movement too, running up his broad chest and back down again.

When Tryn slowed to a stop outside my front door, I didn't even hesitate. "Would you like to come in?" I asked with my chin on his shoulder.

He shut off the bike abruptly and kissed the corner of my mouth over his shoulder. "I'd love to."

The moonlight was bright on my front stoop as I fumbled one-handed to unlock the door, my other hand entangled with Tryn's. When I pushed the door open and looked back at him, his eyes were fixed on the not-quite full moon in the sky.

"It's a beautiful night," I whispered, admiring how the light seemed to outline him in silver.

"Yeah." His gaze returned to me, and he followed me inside. The moment the door closed, he pulled me into his deepest, hungriest kiss yet. "Already the best night I've had in a long time." His lips found my neck and the warm, gentle suction over my pulse catapulted me into a new heightened state of need.

Need him. Need his bite, his claim. Need his teeth and his cock inside me now.

"Wait." I braced my hands against his shoulders, not

pushing him off but freezing up in that position. There was that voice again, that weirdly detached sense that felt like me but *not* me.

"You okay?" Tryn pulled away, his brow was pinched with concern. "Too fast?"

"No. I mean..." Why was I already panting? My body felt tightly wound up like I was building up an orgasm already. And apparently I had some kind of biting kink, which probably wasn't appropriate to broach right before our first time.

Oh God, *our first time.*

Reality hit me like a bucket of ice water to the face. We were about to have sex. I knew on some level all my horniness and desire for touch was about *that,* but I was firmly not in fantasy land anymore. Real sex came with consequences, and not just STDs and surprises nine months later. It came with feelings and vulnerability and being seen naked. And sometimes, never hearing from the person you risked all those consequences to be intimate with.

Gee, was it obvious that I hadn't had sex in years and why?

"Emmaline, we don't have to do anything you're not ready for." Tryn grazed my cheek with his knuckles, the gesture so achingly tender I wanted to melt. "I'm more than happy to just be with you. Doesn't matter what we're doing."

Jesus, he was so *good.* It was like he could see directly into my brain and knew exactly what to say to put my fears at ease. I was terrified of being that vulnerable again, but I also had a deep gut feeling that I could trust him.

"I want to, it's just...been a long time."

"It has for me too." His hand cupped my cheek, fingers

trailing along my neck where he'd just been kissing me. "I don't mind waiting, if that's what you want. I'm, uh," he sucked in a breath like he had to prepare for what to say next, "I'm not seeing anyone else but you."

"Oh." I blinked, having forgotten that people multi-dated. "Okay. Neither am I." As if it wasn't obvious. I wasn't exactly a woman in high demand.

He laughed sheepishly. "It feels weird to say that, but I wanted to make sure you knew. I mean to me, it's obvious." His forehead touched down to mine. "You're so incredible, how could I imagine being with anyone else?"

"Me?" I couldn't stop the shocked laugh that came out.

"Yes, you." His lips brushed my forehead. "I don't know if you're feeling all the same things I am, but this feels right to me. You're brilliant and sweet and I love listening to you. You make me feel lighter, more at ease. So whatever pace you're comfortable with, I'll be here."

In my stunned silence that followed, his hands dropped away and he took a few steps back, a wry half-smile on his lips. "Now, *that* was definitely too much."

"No." I closed the distance between us, reaching on tiptoes to wrap an arm around his neck and kiss him urgently. "No, it wasn't." I kissed him again and again, in between speaking quickly against his mouth. "This feels... amazing. Almost too good to be true. I want you, and I trust you. But I..." I paused for a breath, my lips parted against his. "I think I'm scared of how much I want you. I'm not very experienced, and the last time I did this with someone, it was...not great."

The warm touch of his hand returned to my cheek. "I'm sorry. Do you want to talk about it?"

I shook my head. "Not particularly."

The experience wasn't particularly traumatic, just *bad.* I pushed myself to go to a party in college and hooked up with a guy. He shoved it in with barely any foreplay, never mind any tenderness or care for my pleasure. When he was done, he just...left. And that was the end of it.

Tryn hesitated. "Do you want me to go?"

My lips grazed his with another shake of my head. "No."

Tryn lowered into a crouch, wrapped his arms around my thighs and stood again like I weighed nothing at all. We kissed again while he secured my legs in a straddle around his waist. "Then tell me what you need, beautiful, because as far as I'm concerned, I was put on this earth to please you."

I was so lost for words and floored with emotion, I just poured it all into another kiss. *How can you be real?* I wondered.

"We can take it slow, and just stay cuddled up like this," he suggested. "You can take the lead and tell me exactly what you're craving right now. Whatever you need, I'll give. Or..." he paused and the start of a growl rumbled in his chest. "You can let me take the reins, and I'll do what I've been dying to do since the moment I saw you."

Yes, that, the foreign voice inside me yelled. *Show me your prowess, how strong your animal really is.*

I'd been in a constant push-pull with my desire, my self-control, and this other side of me since Tryn first kissed me. I was tired of fighting my own wants, tired of thinking too much and being afraid to take a real risk.

Despite the voice in my head, the answer I gave was all me.

"Take control of me, Tryn."

CHAPTER 12

EMMALINE

Tryn lifted a brow, the tensions between us taut and simmering. "You're sure?" His voice was low, quiet, but no less thick with desire.

His hesitation had me second-guessing myself. "Well, I don't have condoms—"

"Won't need them." The next thing I knew, he was moving. He carried me through the apartment effortlessly to the bedroom.

"Won't need them?" I repeated right before he lowered me onto the bed, pressing me into the mattress with a deep kiss.

"I'm not fucking you tonight," he rasped against the crook of my neck. "As much as I'd like to."

He lowered himself over me, pulling a gasp from my lips as I felt the solid length of his cock grind against my clit. My thighs snapped like a vice around his hips, urging him to stay.

"Then what—mm..."

His tongue slid against mine as he started small,

shallow thrusts. The friction of our clothes directly over my clit had me squirming, aching for real penetration.

"I can use more than my dick to please you." Tryn smiled against my lips, cocky and not at all nervous. Of course he wasn't, he was a tall, musclebound biker for shit's sake. He'd probably done this thousands of times, with hundreds of different women—

"I love that brain of yours, but don't think so much right now, Emmaline." His next kiss was softer, sweeter. The warm rumble of his voice pulled me right out of my head. "Be here with me, beautiful. Just feel."

Don't think. Feel. The voice in my head echoed what he said.

In an effort to do just that, I barely lifted my head to kiss him again. My eyelids fell closed and I poured all of my focus into feeling Tryn. The softness of his lips contrasted with the roughness of his beard. The heat of him and the breadth of his body. My hands landed on his back and went searching. When I found the hem of his T-shirt, I dipped under it.

Oh, I did not expect his skin to be so soft. The muscles underneath were hard, but also moved with a fluid grace that I never wanted to stop feeling. I already knew he gave great hugs, but to feel him wrap around me skin-to-skin would be on another level.

As if reading my mind, Tryn made off with his shirt when our kisses broke apart for air. When he lowered to me again, his fingers drifted under my shirt slowly, giving me every opportunity to stop him.

I didn't. I kissed him harder, molding my body to his. A strong hand lifted me a few inches from the bed, just enough to get my shirt and bra off.

"Fucking perfect," Tryn murmured along my collarbone before kissing lower.

My gaze found the ceiling. Any other time, I'd be in my head again, wondering if I looked weird topless, if my chest was smaller than what he preferred. But what I was quickly figuring out was that Tryn knew how to make a girl *feel*.

The graze of his teeth on my nipple pulled me right out of my head. That, combined with his hand rolling my other breast, had me arching, pressing into him.

"Does this feel good, Emmaline?" The cocky lift of his lips told me he knew the answer to that already.

"Yes," I whimpered as his tongue and teeth coaxed my nipple into an achingly sensitive peak.

His thumb swept over my other nipple, the edge of his hand stroking the sensitive underside of my breast. God, how did he just *know* every erogenous zone on my body?

That hand began to skim down my body, his palm flat and fingers wide like he didn't want to miss out on touching every part of me he could. He left a trail of heat on my skin, my pulse pounding harder the lower he went. When he reached the top of my jeans he went directly over them, making no attempt to take them off. At least, not right away.

The momentary disappointment I felt was chased away by the pressure he applied between my legs, right where I needed it. My hips shot up from the bed, grinding into his palm like I was possessed. Tryn's hand barely moved but remained firm and steady, molded to the most sensitive area of my body.

"Fuck," he whispered roughly. "I love the sounds you make when you feel good."

Awareness shot back into my body. Sounds? What sounds?

Tryn smothered those thoughts with a deep kiss, his hand rocking insistently between my legs. "Don't start thinking. Just feel. Let me keep making you feel good." He swiftly undid the button and zipper of my jeans, his fingers dipping inside. "I can't wait anymore. I need to know how wet you are."

Letting Tryn take control had been the right choice. He was so sure of himself, so confident in what he wanted. He left me no chance to be self-conscious, no time to get into my own head and wonder about how I looked, sounded, or smelled to him. Every time my thoughts started to spiral, he just made my toes curl with pleasure again.

Just like right then, as he caressed under the layers of my jeans and underwear. His fingers slid over my mound and I wondered if I had done enough grooming down there. Before I could think on it any more, his touch slid over my clit and down further to my core.

"Oh *fuck*." He moaned loudly into the mattress next to my head. "You're soaked. And so hot. I feel like I'll die if I don't taste you."

He kissed me ravenously, tongue thrusting into my mouth like it was a preview of what he was about to do to my pussy. Meanwhile, his hands gripped the edges of my jeans and yanked them down my thighs.

The next thing I knew, I was fully naked while Tryn still had pants on. And still, he didn't allow my thoughts to wander to my various imperfections on display. His body draped gently over mine, warm skin and fluid muscles blanketing me. His kisses turned tender, thick arms sliding around me in an embrace. I held onto the wide expanse of his back, legs sliding apart to hug around his waist.

"You're so stunning," he murmured into my neck before kissing me there.

"You're...magical," I blurted out, at a loss for any better word.

He let out a low chuckle, nipping my throat. "I haven't even done anything yet."

"Not true. You're making me feel *so* good. I've never felt like this with anyone before."

"Neither have I," Tryn whispered before I could wonder if I'd come on too strong.

Our gazes locked in a single intense moment before his lips descended on mine again. The friction of our mouths, the deepening of each kiss, the quick sighs of breaths before finding each other again and again, said everything we weren't ready to put into words yet.

We hadn't known each other long, but every instinct in my body knew there was something here. Something intangible, yet drawing us together in a way that was inescapable. Maybe Tryn *was* the 'something' I had been waiting for.

His touch ran down my body reverently. I shivered as he caressed the sensitive skin of my inner thigh, gently unhooking my leg from his hip. When his fingers stroked my core, my whole body lit up like a live wire.

"I need to taste you so bad but first, I want to see your face when you come." Tryn teased my pussy lips, sliding his fingers through my slick, sensitive folds. "So I guess I just have to make you come twice." He grinned at that, like he would enjoy nothing else more.

I let out a moan when he penetrated me, one blunt

finger stroking inside. His thumb rested over my clit hood, a light, constant pressure made slick by my wetness. Already, he was driving me wild, the sensations so fucking good but not enough. I wanted to be filled up, to have my clit blasted until I had an earth-shaking orgasm around his thick cock.

I wanted to bite him.

And I wanted him to bite me, so fucking bad. The thought of his teeth sinking into me was almost as hot as his cock fucking me.

"Tryn," I whimpered, fingers digging into his back. My whole body nearly levitated off the bed to press against him.

"Mm, Emmaline..."

He added a second finger, rocking them both in and out of me with delicious pressure along my inner walls. Sucking one of my tight, aching nipples into his mouth while his hand steadily fucked me, he was marching me towards the peak, but it still wasn't enough.

I stared at the thick muscle connecting his neck to his shoulder. Fuck, it was the perfect place to bite. I could sink right into the meat, claim him as mine, and come from that alone. This wasn't just a fetish thing, I *needed* to bite him before someone else did.

"Tryn, please..." I was so far gone, so deep in the sensations he brought alive in my body, that I didn't think about the strangeness of my sudden biting urge.

His teeth closed around my nipple with a light pull, and the pleasure, the *rightness* of it, hit me like a lightning strike.

"Yes, please," I begged. "Bite me, bite harder."

My need babbled out, all my shyness gone. But Tryn released the stiff peak with a soft pop of his mouth.

"Another night, Emmaline," he rumbled, kissing my breastbone.

My pleasure and instinct-addled brain never noticed until later how he responded so casually. Like a girl begging for a bite was just normal bedtime activity for him.

"No, now. I need it now." I shook like Jello, on the brink of orgasm under his skilled hand. A bite would make it *so* good, I just knew it would make me come so much harder.

"Next time, my heart. I promise." He sealed that promise with a kiss, pressing me deep into the mattress. "Bitten or not, nothing changes the fact that you are mine."

Hearing that claim from his lips made my heart soar. The words didn't satisfy the way I somehow knew a bite would, but it would do for now.

"You're close, aren't you?" His fist closed in my hair, the other hand fucking me up to his last knuckle, thumb sliding back and forth over my clit. "I can feel that sweet cunt squeezing me."

"Yes," I squeaked on a tight breath, so tightly wound up I thought I might shatter at any moment.

Tryn never sped up or went harder, he just kept up that maddeningly steady pace, marching me closer and closer with each drag and thrust of his fingers.

He never stopped, even when the release burst from me seconds later. My pussy convulsed around him and his fingers spread apart as they stroked in and out, drawing out my pleasure. This utterly selfless, romantic beast of a man kept going until I pushed his hand away, overrun with sensitivity.

And when I did, he brought those fingers to his mouth and moaned as he sucked my juices from them. His eyes heated when they met mine. "I'm not anywhere near done with you, Emmaline."

Jesus Christ, more? My pulse was still thrumming. My lungs ached with the effort to catch my breath. I felt like I sprinted around the block at top speed, and yet completely languid with a sense of ease. For once, my mind was quiet, relaxed. Whatever mental burdens I'd been holding about my job, my family, even my self-consciousness about my body, had fallen away. I was right where I belonged, with the man I belonged with.

So I stretched out long on my bed next to Tryn, soaking up his gaze as it roamed over my naked body, instead of shrinking under it.

"I love seeing you wear nothing but moonlight." He stroked up the side of my body, caressing over my hip and waist. "Never seen anything more beautiful in my life."

I would have swooned if I wasn't already lying down. So I rolled onto my side, facing him and unable to suppress my smile. "How do you always know exactly what to say?"

His smile was soft, his gaze dropping for a moment. "It just comes out when I'm with you. Just feels right."

"It does," I agreed, reaching up to touch the side of his face.

Tryn lowered to kiss me and the low-burning embers of my first orgasm roared to life with renewed heat. He rolled me to my back, and when my arms came around him, he pulled them away and pinned my hands next to my head.

He held me down in several places and I loved it, squirming underneath his body to find more skin-to-skin contact. Fuck, I wish he'd take his pants off. I wanted our legs intertwined and to feel the heated kiss of his cock dragging on my stomach. I *needed* to feel him notch at my core, to hear the growl he'd make as he pressed inside.

But his hips pulled away, and he released my hands to roll my breasts in his large palms, sucking at each of the sensitive tips before his mouth moved lower. I squeezed his sides with my legs, trying to hold him in place but there was no trapping a creature like him.

Tryn moved leisurely down my body, placing kisses on my belly and tracing the edge of my ribcage with his mouth. He just glanced up at me with a smirk when my legs squeezed around him. That heated look promised more in the future. More intimacy, more late night talks in bed, more of what I craved.

When his nose brushed over my mound, he took a deep inhale and moaned. "Fucking moon, this scent."

My clit was so sensitive that I felt the air from his mouth and rumble from his words like they were a tangible touch. I bucked against his mouth without thinking and found my lips captured in his.

"Oh my God!" The declaration burst from me at the torrent of sensations happening between my legs. I'd never received oral before, and *holy fucking shit*.

Tryn kissed me down there just as thoroughly and passionately as he did my mouth. He sucked on me gently, using his tongue to caress and explore. My first orgasm rendered me so sensitive and tender, I felt *everything*. And it was incredible.

He ignored my clit, which I was thankful for at first, but after a few minutes of his incredible mouth, I was desperate for some love there.

I shifted my hips, trying to direct his mouth that way, but the grip he had on my waist was iron-clad. My big bear of a man was intent on feasting and would not be disturbed.

He took a break after some more time, propping up on one elbow as he licked his lips, smiling at me lazily. "Trying to tell me something with all your wiggling?" He placed a kiss on the inside of my knee.

Bite. The word passed through my mind like an insistent command, but I ignored it.

"Aside from the fact that your mouth is amazing?" I panted. "I just, um..." Not only was it hard to come up with words, I didn't want to sound like I was critiquing him.

"Tell me." He placed another kiss higher inside my thigh, slow and sensual. "Tell me exactly what you need."

"I need your mouth, um, higher."

"Where?" He kept his gaze locked on mine, smirking as he kissed my thigh even closer to my core. "Tell me exactly. Or better yet, touch yourself and show me."

Oh God, touching myself? With him looking at me like a hungry wolf?

The spark of fear was undeniable, but so was the exhilaration. Tryn was challenging me to be bold, to be confident in my right to pleasure, to ask for what I wanted. And he made me feel like nothing short of a goddess, so what was there to be afraid of?

"Here." I reached down and touched a finger to my clit hood, beginning a small circular motion.

Tryn smiled widely, showing all of his teeth that, for a blink, looked unusually sharp. "Your wish is my command."

His mouth lowered to the most sensitive part of me, and the first sweep of his tongue sent my hips spiking off the bed.

That tongue, oh *fuck,* his tongue. It slid over that hard

bundle of nerves with the most exquisite pressure. His lips sucked gently around it, and my second orgasm began coiling up like a spring.

When he added his fingers to stroke and curl inside me once again, I knew it would be mere seconds.

"Don't stop," I chanted breathlessly, my hands clenched in his hair and my pussy grinding shamelessly against his mouth. "Oh my fucking God, please don't stop…"

Each lash of his tongue on my clit, every pump of his fingers into me, was like the tapping of a hammer against glass. Every strike of pleasure lighting up my spine made a crack in that glass pane. The cracks spread, spiderwebbing outward until they were all I could feel.

And then finally, I shattered and came apart. It was even more explosive than the last one, my body convulsing uncontrollably as the high swept over me.

Just like before, Tryn drew out my pleasure with his tongue and fingers until I came down, nerves frayed and completely sated.

Tryn placed a kiss on my lower belly and wordlessly crawled up the bed to lie next to me. I turned to him, snuggling into his chest. With the heat of my orgasm, his skin felt cooler than normal.

"What about you?" I murmured against his throat.

"Don't worry about me. I'm good." He kissed my forehead, running a hand down my spine. "I just wanted to take care of you tonight."

"Hm…"

He laughed, embracing me tighter. "You're half asleep anyway."

"S'your fault."

"I take full responsibility."

I drifted off feeling more warm, satisfied, and relaxed than I ever had before. But too soon, I was being roused with kisses on my cheek and neck, my shoulder being shaken gently.

"Emmaline," I heard Tryn whisper. "I have to go."

"What?" I rubbed my eyes, confusion bringing me to wakefulness. "What time is it?"

"Just after midnight."

I blinked, my eyes adjusting to the sight of Tryn fully dressed and standing next to my bed.

"You're…leaving?" I stared at him, my hurt and confusion mounting.

"I'm sorry. I really wish I could stay, but I can't." He bent and kissed me quickly, a complete one-eighty from his usual long, lingering kisses. "I'll call you soon, okay?"

Soon. Not tomorrow. Not in the morning. Just a vague, non-committal *soon*.

"I don't understand." All kinds of alarm bells rang inside me, multiple instincts and gut feelings screaming that this was not right. "Why do you need to rush off in the middle of the night?"

Tryn sucked in a breath, hesitating before answering. "I had an emergency come up with work. Trust me, I'd much rather not leave but I can't get out of this."

"And you can't tell me what the emergency is."

His gaze hardened, shutting me out firmly. "Not yet. I'm sorry."

I pulled the covers up to my chin, suddenly feeling cold, exposed, and hurt. Not to mention extremely wary of the man I thought I trusted. "Well, I guess I better not keep you."

He didn't try to kiss me again, but instead headed

straight for the front door. "Promise I'll call you," he yelled before closing it behind him.

I didn't go back to sleep. I laid there, in the bed where he pleased me so well, with my knees tucked into my chest and my mind racing. The memory of what we'd done felt tainted now.

I wondered if I'd made a colossal mistake.

CHAPTER 13

EMMALINE

Tryn didn't call the next day. Or the day after. After three days of not hearing from him, I caved and called him.

He never picked up.

Work kept me busy up to a point. Annika and Joey could immediately tell something was up. After some goading, I ended up confessing to them what had happened between Tryn and me. Those two were the closest thing I had to friends, after all.

"He's probably married, like you thought at the beginning," Annika said, viciously stabbing a receipt onto the check spindle.

"Even if he's not married, he's hiding something," Joey agreed. "I mean, he pretty much told you that straight out, but the job thing's got to be bullshit."

The job thing was just such a convenient excuse, and not a great one at that. What could have possibly happened that he had to dash off in the middle of the night?

On my next day off, I was on a walk on the trail around

my apartment, as though keeping my body busy would help to forget what he'd done to me.

I wanted to be angry. I wanted to find that confidence he drew out of me in the bedroom and use it to stand up to his lies. I wanted to find him and demand the truth. Didn't I deserve that, at least?

But the truth was, I was deeply hurt. I felt rejected. Not good enough. My biggest fear was that he left my bed that night to crawl into someone else's, and I wondered why he'd choose her over me. What did I do wrong? Why wasn't I enough?

I rubbed my chest as I walked, trying to soothe the permanent ache that seemed to settle there since he left. It felt like our connection had been a thread between us, at first strong and tethering, drawing us closer together. But him leaving had unraveled that thread, stretched it beyond the limit of its strength, and now it was frayed and damaged.

On top of all that, I was also ridiculously horny, which didn't help things.

The morning after Tryn left, I'd forgotten for a moment and reached for him in bed. Before my eyes opened, I had a smile on my lips. He'd probably enjoy waking up to a blowjob. I still had a piece of that confident sex goddess he'd drawn out of me, and I was more than prepared to take him into my mouth. Maybe then he'd be unable to resist fucking me. He'd drag me up his body until I was straddling him. He'd penetrate me deep, bouncing me on his cock while his teeth found my neck...

But the bed was cold, empty. And the night before came rushing back to me. His goodbye probably took under a minute, and I replayed every word in my head. Every 'sorry', every moment of eye contact and when he looked away. The one conclusion I kept returning to was that he was being dishonest.

Despite knowing that and feeling so wounded from it, I couldn't stop craving him physically.

I wrung orgasm after orgasm out of myself, using my one trusty vibrator, my fingers, the showerhead, everything. And it was never enough. I couldn't even get there unless I was thinking of him.

I felt pathetic and lovesick, because I really was starting to fall for him. I wanted to howl my lungs out with all the frustration and pain of rejection, the utter fucking loneliness in his absence.

"What's happening to me?" I asked the question with my face turned up to the shower, the water running cold. This wasn't *me*. I didn't fall apart over men like this. But then again, I'd never fallen this hard for one either.

No answer came from the running water, but I knew something in me had fundamentally changed since meeting Tryn. I had never been this pathetic over a guy before, never been so convinced that he could be the one for me and then so shattered when I turned out to be wrong.

"Maybe I just need therapy." I shut the shower off.

My bedroom was bathed in silver from the full moon that night, bright as any street lamp outside my window. I tried not to think about how Tryn called me beautiful when I wore nothing but the moon's light.

Strangely, the moon gave me an odd sense of comfort as I crawled into bed. Something about that round rock in the sky filled me with enough peace that I started drifting off to sleep, an assurance that this was just one of the many cycles in my life.

When morning came, the loneliness rushed in just as fiercely as it had in the days before. The ache in my chest wasn't as sharp, but that didn't make me feel better. It felt like I'd been sleeping under a block of ice and had gone numb.

I reached for my phone before I was even fully awake and hit the call button next to Tryn's number without any of the clarity or resolve from the night before. I might have had the book smarts to call myself a doctor, but in this, I was a painfully slow learner.

The answer became clear to me though, as his phone rang and rang without getting picked up.

CHAPTER 14

TRYN

Emmaline should be here. That was my constant thought as I ran with my pack under the full moon. The moon I would rather curse out than howl at in that moment. It was because of the moon that I had to tear myself away from Emmaline, after all.

An hour after we began, Derric scented a buck and our run soon became a hunting party. Five of us took down the prey, but it was Sawyer who gave the killing strike to the windpipe. Once the buck lay dead, our pack howled a song of victory. Sawyer would take the biggest share of the meat and present it to his pregnant mate, proving himself a capable provider and protector.

I wasn't normally an envious wolf. That kind of bitterness wasn't my style, but I found Sawyer's happy howls and barks grating my ears. His playful roughhousing with our packmates to burn off his remaining adrenaline seemed childish and obnoxious to me.

Any other time, I'd be proud of him. Our lone, prickly enforcer, a brother to me, had become a family man. He was settled, content. In love with his mate and excited for his pup to arrive.

It was only because my mate wasn't at my side, because I had to leave her soft bed and warm body to be here, that I had these ugly, bitter thoughts. The human side of me knew that. But my wolf was a creature of instinct, not reason, and he wouldn't stop sulking.

We left her alone just before the moon's full strength without a bite, even though she begged us for it, he kept reminding me. *We did not give our mate what she needed. We failed her.*

There will be another full moon. She needs time to understand what we are. I tried to soothe him, but my animal was not having it.

If she hasn't moved on to another male already, my wolf huffed. *A male who will not deceive her, who will treat her exactly as she deserves.*

My wolf wasn't wrong about that. Emmaline did deserve better than someone who lied about who he was and left her bed in the middle of the night. But when the moon was full, and the shift therefore yanked out of my control, how would she feel about the man in her bed turning into a huge, four-legged predator?

She thinks I'm handsome, my wolf reminded me. *Let me go see her.*

And risk you biting her? No.

My wolf let out a frustrated growl. *She* wanted *our bite.*

She didn't know what she was asking for.

My inner beast remained sullen and argumentative. He couldn't understand that Emmaline had a whole life as a human. She was destined for a fulfilling career as a veterinarian. Even if she didn't react poorly to finding out what I was, what *she* most likely was, she might not want a life as a shifter. I couldn't just bite her and let the pieces fall where they may. I liked her too much, respected her too much, to take that choice away from her.

Even if she didn't choose me.

The thought of Emmaline *not* choosing me made my wolf absolutely feral with rage and hurt. I had to break away from the pack for a while and run a few laps through the woods so that I wouldn't inadvertently attack a packmate.

Such was the way of being a shifter, always trying to balance your animal and human sides. The full moon put the animal in charge for one night, forcing the human side to take a backseat. It took all my effort to draw my wolf away from expressing his anguish in a violent way.

By the time I returned to the pack, the moon had passed its peak in the sky. Its magic that had tightened its grip on us for the last several days had loosened again, allowing our human sides more control.

Everyone was gathered around the pond, the same one Emmaline and I had seen on our first date. It was cute that she had called it a lake.

About half the pack was still in wolf form, relaxing on the pond's shores or gnawing on some bone of the buck we brought down. Those who had returned to their human forms either relaxed in the grassy meadow or had waded into the water for a quick wash.

We were all as naked as the day we were born, and no one cared. Nudity was natural, whether you were animal or human. Although some couples had snuck off to the taller grasses of the meadow or to the cover of trees. The moon's magic was also responsible for hormone surges and increases in fertility. More pups might be conceived tonight.

Sawyer had shifted back to his human form and stood in a waist-deep area of the pond. I approached the area of shore closest to him as he washed the buck's blood from his mouth, neck, and chest.

"Good kill," I told him once I had a human mouth. Being a human felt better right then, even though I was envious of him. My wolf was too volatile at the moment.

"Thanks." He splashed water on his face, then raked his fingers back through his hair. "Couldn't have done it without you diving for his legs like that. I thought you'd get trampled."

I shrugged. I did get some hoof kicks in my ribs, but it was no big deal. They'd bruise for a day or two, then heal away.

"Did you get your portion?" Sawyer emerged from the water and sat on the grassy shore next to me.

"Nah. I'll get some cuts at the lodge when we butcher properly. How's Riley feeling?" I needed a subject change, one that wasn't focused on me.

His brow creased with worry. "Shifting has been making her nauseous, so I told her to stay home and rest tonight. Literally everyone is telling me the nausea is normal, but I just hate to see her suffer."

"It'll pass. Anyway, she's strong. She's been through worse."

He nodded, leaning back on his elbows as he stared pensively across the water. "I'll take a rack of ribs, I think, and make a stew for her. Something easy on her stomach."

"Have you talked to Shiloh?"

"Yeah. Riley's got a big pot of this enchanted tea from her. She says it's been helping."

"That's good. She's going to be a great mother."

That got a smile out of him. His teeth, still pointed and slightly wolflike, shined as brightly as the moonlight. "Yeah, she is. I can't wait." He nudged me with his elbow. "How's it going with your mate?"

I sighed. This was the question I'd been hoping to avoid. "I don't know, to be honest."

"Well, what's up?"

How the tables had turned. I was usually the listening ear for my packmates, and look at me now.

"Things were going well, I think. But I...I had to leave her a couple days ago. Late at night after we'd, you know."

"So you wouldn't bite her," he concluded. "I take it you didn't go all the way, then?"

I stared at him. Not exactly in surprise but in stark relief and solidarity. Of course he knew, he'd been through the same thing. "Yes, exactly. And no, we didn't. She was begging for a bite and my jaw fucking ached from how hard I clenched it to keep it closed."

Sawyer licked his lips and smiled, a faraway look coming to his eyes. "The first time I went down on Riley, it was so I wouldn't be tempted to use my teeth on her. When you're tasting the most intimate part of a woman, your instincts shift to being gentle with her."

"Yes!" I agreed. "I swear that's the only reason I didn't end up biting her. And that's why I had to leave, I couldn't risk sleeping next to her. Or freak her out by potentially shifting in my sleep."

Sawyer chuckled. "I've never been much of a sleep-shifter. Riley is though, it's very cute. Half the time I wake up in the morning, I'm snuggling her wolf instead of her."

Another pang of jealousy hit me. I wanted those little domestic moments with Emmaline, those quirks unique only to our relationship.

"It doesn't happen often for me, but enough to the point where it's not worth the risk."

"So she doesn't know anything yet?"

I shook my head. "I don't know how to broach it. She's so...very human."

"Hmm." Sawyer cocked his head in thought. Riley had been kidnapped from the human world by vampires, so by the time Sawyer found her, she had already known about werewolves to some degree.

"I don't know, Tryn," he said apologetically. "That might be a band-aid you just have to rip off. She wanted your bite, so I figure that's a positive sign she has a wolf inside her. Riley and Aria experienced the same thing."

"Gran said that wasn't a big enough sample size to tell. It could just be the fate thread wanting to seal the deal."

Sawyer made a dismissive sound. "Gran and her sample sizes."

"And then there's Shiloh," I pointed out. "She has a bite from Orson, but she's not of our species."

"Hmm, yeah. True." Sawyer looked thoughtfully out at the water. "When she and I were together, I was never tempted to bite her. So maybe it's more of a mate thing than a wolf thing."

I had almost forgotten that Sawyer and Shiloh had a brief, casual relationship. It wasn't that long ago but since finding their mates, it felt like ancient history. While they had been dating, I had seen their fate threads leading away from each other, but it wasn't my place to get involved. Mated pairs seemed to find each other whenever the moon deemed it was time.

"All I know is I can't keep lying to Emmaline." I scratched my beard. "Leaving her like I did really hurt her and...I can't do that to her again. I want her to trust me."

"Listen to you," Sawyer teased. "Already such a good mate. I hope she knows how lucky she is."

"Shut up," I grumbled.

He gave me a few good-natured slaps on the back. "Anything the pack can do for you, let us know. Anything to help fate along."

"Actually." An idea started forming. One that might be the perfect compromise. "Maybe there is something."

"Spill it."

"At the lodge," I countered.

Dawn had broken by the time the pack gathered at our home base. I approached Derric first, then together, he and I presented it to the pack at large. They were overwhelmingly supportive. Orson would only have to check in with his mate, Shiloh, but he expressed that she would be on board as well.

Feeling lighter and more hopeful, I returned to my room to get a few hours of much-needed sleep. After picking up my phone from the bedside table, I swore under my breath at the sight of two missed calls from Emmaline.

I hit the button to call her back and pressed the phone to my ear. My heart sank lower and lower as the ringing went on with no answer.

CHAPTER 15

EMMALINE

I left my phone at home on my next day off so that I wouldn't be tempted to check it, or worse, try calling Tryn for a third time. My persistent ache for him was stronger than my pride, although I successfully did not check my phone at all during my shift last night. It stayed buried at the bottom of my purse where it belonged.

When I got home, I took the phone out—without looking at the screen—and stashed it in my sock drawer, hoping all the fabric would muffle any vibrations enough for me to not hear.

Not that I expected him to call me, anyway. But stupidly, I still hoped.

I went about my errands as normally as I could; grocery shopping, dropping bills off at the post office, and spending a few hours with my laptop in a coffee shop applying to more vet residencies.

At least I was at a more reasonable level of horny after that full moon night. I knew the moon cycles didn't really affect hormone levels, but it was easier to blame my insane sex drive that night on temporary lunacy than the real reason.

The reason being I still wanted and craved the man who swept me off my feet, only to leave me in the middle of the night like a booty call. And then completely ghosted me afterwards.

The last person I expected to see waiting at my doorstep when I got home was that very same man.

I never actually reached the doorstep. From several yards away, I saw Tryn sitting there in a contemplative pose, forearms on his knees and fingers laced, staring at his hands. I had stopped short, grocery bags in hand, and couldn't believe what I was seeing.

A few seconds passed before he looked up. I didn't know if he heard me or just sensed me there, but for once, he didn't smile as he stood and approached me.

"Hey," he said softly, holding out his hand. "Let me take those for you."

My brain stuttered back to life at the low, warm timbre of his voice. What I wanted to do was press my cheek to the center of his chest and listen to the lazy rumble of his voice throughout my whole body. Instead, I stuck my arms out to thrust the grocery bags at him.

If he ditched and ghosted me, the least he could do was carry my heavy stuff.

Tryn took the bags without a word and followed me to my front door, which I unlocked and left wide open for him to follow me inside. He set the bags on the counter, then stood awkwardly as I started unloading. He was the one who showed up, so he could do the talking.

"I, uh." He scratched his beard, watching me. "I tried to call."

"You did?" I paused, trying to tamp down the elation soaring in my chest. "When?"

"Early this morning. And then an hour ago. Sorry to just show up unannounced, but I got worried."

I put down the coffee creamer I'd been holding and turned to face him. "I've been busy with work and haven't kept track of my phone. I must have left it here when I went out." It wasn't a total lie, plus I wanted to save a little bit of my pride. No way was I going to admit I'd been glued to my phone, waiting to hear from him, if I hadn't stashed it away.

"Okay," Tryn said uneasily.

The tension in his body, his nervous glances, everything screamed that he knew he'd done something wrong. He looked guilty.

"I called *you*, though."

"I know. I'm sorry I didn't return them sooner."

"Couldn't let the wife hear you, huh?"

The barb lashed out of my mouth without thought, but fuck it. I was tired of people thinking I was meek and could be so easily pushed around. My parents tried. Dr. Marcus and Dr. Stone tried. Tryn would not be the one to pull the wool over my eyes.

He rocked back like I'd slapped him, dark eyes narrowing. "What?"

"Your wife." Now that my suspicion was out there, I might as well go all in. "Or your live-in girlfriend, boyfriend, whoever you're hiding."

"I don't have a *wife*." Tryn ground his molars on the word. "There's no one but you, Emmaline. I told you I wasn't seeing anyone else."

"Really?" A sarcastic laugh burst out of my mouth. "You

expect me to believe that? When you're so clearly hiding something?"

He sighed heavily, pinching his nose bridge like he was trying to take the edge off a migraine. "You're right," he said, looking at me intently again. "I haven't been honest with you about everything. I came here to apologize and come clean. But the one thing I've *never* lied about is how I feel for you."

I wanted to believe him. That invisible thread in my chest ached like it was trying to pull me toward him, into his arms and against that thick, warm chest. But still, I hesitated. He would not take me for a fool.

"Go ahead, then." I folded my arms, trying to keep my voice flat. "Come clean. What haven't you been honest about?"

Tryn hesitated. "It would be better if I showed you."

"Showed me?"

He nodded. "Well first thing is, I'm not from Canada. But I am from a place called Vargmore that's not too far from here. It's not on any map though, and you're not likely to find it unless you know how. What I told you about it being a hidden, close-knit community was completely true." He extended a palm toward me. "I don't want anything hidden between us, so I'd like to take you there. To show you my home and family."

I stared at his hand and then at his face. "You're still not telling me everything. The night you left. Your work emergency wasn't true, right?"

Tryn inhaled as if bracing himself. "Right. I'll explain about that too. But it's a…lot of information to take in. I don't want to overwhelm you right away. Can I show you my home first, and then we can talk about my job?"

I shook my head, not in a way that was saying no, but more in a sense of disbelief. "What *haven't* you lied about?"

"My feelings for you," he answered in a low growl. "I swear, Emmaline. Every minute I'm away from you, I'm dying to be at your side. I want a future for us, and I've fucking hated lying to you about my life. More than anything, I want you to be able to trust me, and I have so much fucking regret that we started off with lies, but…" He hesitated for a long time. "After I show you everything, I hope you can understand why I couldn't be honest from the start. I swear to you, I never would have lied unless it was for a damn good reason."

What reason could there possibly be? My mind started going wild with possibilities. Was he in witness protection or something? What were the odds of that?

He looked so earnest, so sincere. The strange part of me that seemed to awaken whenever he was near, urged, *Give him a chance. Let him show you his truth.* And my heart, the part of myself that I knew well, wanted to do the same. What harm would it do to hear him out? If I continued to have even a whiff of suspicion after he laid everything on the table, I could still walk away.

"Okay," I heard myself say. "Are we taking your bike?"

Tryn blinked as if he couldn't believe what I'd said but recovered quickly. "Um, yes. It'll be about a two-hour ride, so dress warm."

"Alright." My attention returned to the groceries on the counter. "Help me put these away first?"

We made quick work of tidying up, then Tryn went to warm up his bike while I put more layers on.

"Am I stupid?" I wondered, continuing the trend of talking out loud that was going so well for me.

Not stupid. Fair and caring, the other side of me answered. I had gotten used to this other voice, to the point where I found it comforting. Like a friend inside my head that was always listening.

"Maybe crazy and stupid," I said as I shrugged a jacket on. I really needed to find a residency program. Then I'd have health insurance and would be able to see a neurologist about this. Voices in your head weren't normal. And I'd never heard anything besides my own thoughts until recently.

Until Tryn.

Which was most likely a coincidence. Auditory hallucinations, among other symptoms of schizophrenia, often didn't show up until people were in their thirties. What was strange, though, was that I hadn't developed any other symptoms of mental illness. No paranoia, major mood swings, memory loss, depression, or mania. It was just a voice, and a sense of feelings and wants separate from my own, but also interwoven with my own emotions and desires.

I found it all very curious but not at all alarming.

Tryn's motorcycle rumbled with a low, steady growl while I locked up and headed over to join him on the metal beast. A sigh left my mouth the moment I settled behind him, and I was grateful that he couldn't hear it over the engine. It felt so right being here, even though I'd only ridden with him a handful of times.

My arms felt like they belonged around his waist. His broad back was the perfect support for my cheek or forehead to rest on. Wrapping around him felt like we were two puzzle pieces locking together. The ache in my chest immediately soothed into a gentle, warm glow.

He didn't touch my legs as he drove, and while I was grateful that he respected the boundaries I had established in my hurt, I fiercely missed him touching me the way he used to.

God, I hope this all makes sense, I prayed. *I hope the truth comes out and he really is the same person I'm falling for.*

CHAPTER 16

TRYN

As eager as I was to show Vargmore to Emmaline, I never wanted the ride to end. It felt right, having her on the bike with me, holding onto me as we leaned into the turns. Our fate thread sparked brightly, as if pleased with our reunion.

This was how we were meant to be. Together. Winding through mountain roads on a motorcycle in our human forms, and, if she had an animal side, running through the dense trees in our wolf forms.

All I had to do was unfuck everything I'd fucked up.

After about an hour of riding, I turned off the main road onto a barely-marked gravel road. The kind of road no one saw unless it was exactly what they were looking for.

This road was narrow and even more twisty than the highway. Emmaline never voiced a single complaint. She trusted me enough to see this through, at least.

I drove for another hour before we crossed the metaphysical border between Shyftworld and the human world. It was barely noticeable, like a featherlight brush against my skin. I found it funny that Emmaline had thought it was a spiderweb on our first date.

This road was the main passage I used to cross between worlds, although the path to the lookout spot I'd taken her to was another. It was harder to get to town from the lookout spot though, and town was the first place I wanted to bring Emmaline to explain.

The forest eventually thinned out to a clearing, where Stout & Spirit greeted us cheerily from the horizon. A fleet of motorcycles were parked outside, just as we'd planned. My heart pounded in anticipation as I pulled up next to Ruse's bike and parked.

This was it. My two worlds colliding.

I let Emmaline off first, holding my arm out to support her, before dismounting myself.

"Welcome to Vargmore." I held an arm out toward the tavern's front door, hoping my smile didn't look as nervous as I felt. "This is our first stop. Our local watering hole."

Emmaline gazed up at the brick building with its tall, slanted roof, weathered copper weathervane of a wolf chasing a rooster, red-bricked chimney, and wrought-iron sign above the door.

"So," Emmaline looked behind her at the road and forest and then at the tavern again, "where exactly *are* we? Is this even California anymore? Planet Earth?"

"We're not in California." I kept my voice level, hoping to keep her from getting too freaked out. "Or the United States. As for the same planet, I don't honestly know. Shyftworld is what most of us call this place as a whole. Our known world, so to speak. Vargmore is the territory I live in. From what we've observed, Shyftworld exists parallel to your world, with some overlaps here and there."

"Another world," she repeated. "Like another dimension. A parallel universe, maybe?"

"Something like that." I watched her carefully, noting her lack of emotion. Maybe she was in shock. "Are you okay?"

Emmaline blinked, then smoothed her hair back with a sigh. "I don't know. This is a lot and I'm trying to process. But I keep thinking back to lectures in school where they said parallel universes are theoretically possible. So, my brain isn't totally broken yet."

I kept staring at her face, concern making me hyper aware of every twitch and micro-expression. "Do you want to go back?"

"No. No, I'm good. We're already here." She focused on Stout & Spirit's weathervane again. "This place is really cute. Charming, actually. Reminds me of those old European pubs that have been around since the middle ages."

The building probably was that old, but that wasn't information she needed to be bothered with yet.

"Wait until you see the inside." I grabbed the heavy iron handle and pulled the front door open for her. She didn't see it, but I sucked in an apprehensive breath before swinging my gaze to the inside.

"Hello, welcome!" Shiloh called from behind the bar. "Please come in."

All was normal, and I let the breath out in a sigh of relief. My packmates were gathered around their tables, drinks in hand, in human form and fully dressed. Convincing them to wear clothing was half the battle, honestly.

"Have a seat anywhere you'd like. I'm Shiloh." The

witch and owner of the tavern turned up the charm, smiling brightly at Emmaline. "Tryn has told us so much about you."

"He has?" Emmaline turned to look over her shoulder at me, but her gaze bounced around at all the werewolves. Her human instincts must have been on high alert, and for good reason. She was in a room full of not only strangers but predators.

"He won't *stop* talking about you," Sawyer called from his booth in the corner. His arm was around Riley's shoulders and he too, smiled at my mate, though his teeth were a little sharp. He probably didn't even realize it. Male wolves were a whole new level of protective when their mates were pregnant.

"I'm Riley, and this is Sawyer." Said pregnant mate gave a little pat to Sawyer's chest. "Your man and mine have been causing trouble since they were old enough to run."

"Just as best friends are meant to." Sawyer kissed her temple, his free hand coming to rest on her belly.

"Nice to meet you both," Emmaline said, casting another glance back at me. "I've heard some stories about this childhood troublemaking."

Riley rolled her eyes and smiled earnestly at my mate. "Not half of them, I'm sure. They're epic sagas if you ask this one." She scratched under Sawyer's jaw.

I touched Emmaline's shoulder. "How about we get a drink, and then you can meet everybody else?"

"Oh, sure." She proceeded into the tavern until she reached the bar, bringing her hands hesitantly to the long slab of polished wood. Orson was in the seat next to her, and when he turned his icy gaze to Emmaline, I held my breath for the second time.

Orson was a good guy. Loyal and extremely intelligent. But if there was one thing he lacked, it was social skills.

"Hi," he said abruptly, sticking his hand out toward her. "I'm Orson."

There was only a moment of hesitation before she smiled with enough warmth to melt even his icy demeanor. "Emmaline," she returned, clasping his hand. "It's nice to meet you."

"You as well. That's a pretty name."

My wolf was growling, pawing under my skin at the compliment, even though the human side of me knew he didn't intend to be flirtatious.

"Thank you. You have stunning eyes, by the way. I hope you don't mind me saying."

Orson grinned, his arctic blues shining like diamonds, and then he winked at her. "Thanks."

My growl was audible this time, and my packmate only snickered at my possessiveness. Across the bar, his mate, Shiloh, rolled her eyes.

"Be careful," she told Emmaline. "Too many compliments about his eyes will go to his head."

"I only did that to mess with Tryn." Orson turned toward me, one arm relaxing on the back of his barstool. "We never get to see Mr. Easy Going all wound up."

"I'm not wound up." Even as I said that, my hand fell to Emmaline's shoulder. Everyone in the room had already picked up my scent on her, but it wasn't enough. I wanted them to *see* that she was mine.

Then you should bite her, my wolf said irritably.

"What can I get you?" Shiloh's friendly tone eased the tension in my shoulders. "Tryn mentioned you liked Irish reds. I don't have one on tap at the moment, but I have a red IPA that's excellent."

"Oh, sure." Emmaline nodded. "I'll have that."

"Two," I added. "Thanks, Shiloh."

"You got it. We've got flatbreads coming out of the oven shortly if you're hungry. Love, will you go check on them?"

"Yes." Orson leaned across the bar and kissed her quickly before heading around and through the back door.

Emmaline and I had just received our beers when Derric walked up. The Alpha kept a sizable distance from her, probably so as not to appear threatening. Normal humans could still feel the distinct air of dominance from an Alpha werewolf, even if they didn't know exactly what it was.

"Nice to meet you, Emmaline. I'm Derric." He gave a little wave since he wasn't close enough to shake hands. "Hope you don't mind all the curious glances. We don't get many visitors in Vargmore."

She smiled at him. "Oh, it's alright." I could scent her nervousness, but she was putting on a brave face and it made me swell with pride. "So, Derric. You're the minor celebrity, right?"

The Alpha slid a glance at me, a smirk popping at the corner of his mouth. "Yeah, that's right."

Emmaline nodded and some of her nerves disappeared. She'd noticed I hadn't lied about him. "You're the important person he has to protect," she went on.

"Sort of." Derric didn't miss a beat. "I'm the leader of our little community here. So this pack of animals, including your man," he swept his arm to indicate everyone in the tavern, "is all about protecting our home, Vargmore. And I guess I'm an extension of that." He flashed a grin. "Although I like to think I can handle myself."

Most of his scars were hidden underneath his hair or clothing, but they were testaments to Derric's strength as an Alpha. He'd remained our pack leader because everyone who challenged him for it had either died or limped away from the battle with their tail between their legs.

"And what *is* Vargmore, exactly?" Emmaline looked at me and then back at Derric. "I get the sense that it's hidden and somewhat cut off from the rest of the world, but can I ask why?"

"That's a great question." Derric focused a hard look at me, a clear sign that I should be the one to answer.

I placed a light hand on Emmaline's back. "Let's go out back where I can show you."

She gave me a puzzled glance but nodded and allowed me to lead her out a side door. The side and back area of the tavern was clear of any trees, with gravel covering the ground. This area was where Shiloh parked her car, accepted deliveries for the tavern, and where the spiral staircase led up to her apartment on the second level. I guided Emmaline to a small table with two chairs set up under an awning, facing the woods at the edge of the clearing.

"What did you want to show me—oh my God!"

Right on cue, two wolves emerged from the treeline, bounding straight for us. Their mouths were open in toothy smiles, tongues lolling out. They ran, not as predators hunting prey, but as friends coming to greet us.

"It's okay," I told Emmaline with a hand on her arm. "They're not aggressive."

Fallon, the bigger of the two wolves, stopped a few yards away and sat on his haunches. He let out a short howl, tail thumping on the ground. His mate, Aria, came closer, approaching Emmaline with bright, curious eyes.

"Are these...*wild* wolves?" Emmaline remained completely still.

"In a sense. You can let her sniff you. She won't bite."

I almost thought she wouldn't, but my brave mate slowly put her hand out toward Aria's dark nose. The female wolf sniffed and licked her hand, then pressed her forehead into Emmaline's palm.

Emmaline jerked her hand back like she'd been burned. "They can't be wild. She's asking for pets."

"These wolves are...different." I had recited so many explanations in my head for this moment, but nothing else sounded quite right. "They have regular contact with humans but they can still fend for themselves."

Fallon had come up to my chair at that point and rested his chin on my arm, staring up at me with big puppy eyes.

"Hi there, buddy." I gave his forehead a scratch and whispered so that only the wolves could hear me. "Thanks for doing this, guys."

"So...you protect the wolves that live here, in this place where you grew up?" Emmaline tentatively stroked one of Aria's ears and the she-wolf's eyes half-closed in utter delight.

"Yes. Ow." Fallon had playfully bitten me and I yanked my hand away, giving him a glare. "That's exactly what we do here."

"So you're like conservationists?"

"Sort of. It's more than a job, though. It's...our way of life. We protect our home and these wolves with our lives. And we're not bound by any government or laws. Derric's word is the law here."

"I see." Emmaline was full-on scratching Aria's scruff now, her fear melting away.

And the wolf loved the attention, so much so that her mate was becoming jealous. Fallon left my side with a huff and went over to his mate, where he licked and nuzzled her snout.

"Are these two a mated pair?" Emmaline watched the wolves' affection with a small smile.

"Yes. This is Aria and Fallon." Both wolves' ears twitched at the sounds of their names, which Emmaline noticed.

"Wow. They have names and even respond to them."

"Yes. The wolves have every right to be here, just as we do. It was their home long before any humans arrived. So we treat them with respect, with dignity, as we do humans."

Every word I told her was the truth, even though she was hearing me from a different perspective. Watching her intently, I wondered if anything was clicking inside her, if she'd ever arrived at the thought that humans and wolves could be one and the same. If she had a wolf inside, was her animal talking to her yet? Explaining her dual nature?

Emmaline's face was thoughtful, curious, as she petted the wolves. If she had any wild notions of humans turning into wolves, she didn't show it.

"The wolf I hit with my car," she said after a few quiet minutes. "These wolves remind me of him. He was clearly wild but could be so docile. The body composition looks similar too, although he was bigger than this guy."

Fallon let out an annoyed huff and Aria playfully nipped her mate. I'd specifically asked these two to approach Emmaline in their wolf forms because they were younger, and therefore smaller in stature. Fallon might reach my size one day, but it was doubtful anyone would get bigger than Derric.

Derric's wolf, the huge and battle-scarred Alpha, was terrifying, even to other werewolves. Even someone as fearless as Emmaline would have run screaming at the sight of him. Sawyer, Orson, and Ruse were risky gambles as well. Not as big as Derric but the size of them could be intimidating.

So that left Fallon, who was always a good sport. Because of Aria, I had a feeling he had a soft spot for humans-slash-latent werewolves. And he'd never say no to head scratches.

"Your wolf may be from here," I hedged carefully. "The wolves of this territory don't often leave. But it's been known to happen." *Such as when they're following the threads of fate.*

"I hope he's from here." Emmaline leaned back, taking a break from all the petting. "If he is, then I'm especially glad I released him when I did." She shot me a guilty look. "I didn't tell you before, but I may have done it kind of illegally."

"Emmaline!" I said in a mock gasp of shock. "You? Doing something *illegal?*"

"I know." She laughed. "But my colleague wanted him kept and examined. I just...couldn't let that happen. If they had done that and then found this place?" She shook her head. "They'd bring tons of scientists through here, and then the government and private companies would want a piece. Vargmore would be...defiled. And your way of life would be gone. That would be such a tragedy."

"Yeah, we're very protective of this place," I said. "We

prefer not to resort to violence, though we are prepared to do so if we must. If fucking armies came through here, though?" I shook my head. "We wouldn't stand a chance. So yeah, probably a good thing you illegally released that wolf."

Emmaline laughed lightly and we sat in comfortable silence for a while. Aria and Fallon lie on a patch of grass nearby, nuzzling and grooming each other. A fierce ache tugged at my chest, and I looked down to see my fate thread practically vibrating. It tugged me toward Emmaline with an almost violent pull.

I know, I thought, rubbing my chest. Human affection was nice enough, but I wanted it all with her. I wanted to groom her fur and feel the playful nip of her wolf's teeth just as much as I wanted to feel her wrapped around me on the motorcycle.

She was in my world now, the truth slowly trickling in. We were getting closer to full, complete honesty, and that made me hopeful.

"So, what do you think of all this?" I asked.

Emmaline looked away from Fallon and Aria chasing each other across the clearing. "I think this place is amazing." She gave me a wry smile. "I'm a little jealous you got to grow up in a place like this. It's like a dream. Or a fairytale." After a slight pause she added, "I think I understand why you weren't forthright with everything. This place is... precious. It needs to be protected. I'm still not thrilled about the dishonesty, but I can see why you felt the need for it."

"Thank you. I really wanted you to see Vargmore for yourself." It was more forgiveness than I expected, or probably even deserved, but from her, I would take it.

CHAPTER 17

EMMALINE

It was near dark by the time Tryn took me home. At one point on the ride back, I felt a distinct sensation over my skin, like invisible fabric passing over me. I wondered if this was the overlap between worlds that Tryn had mentioned.

While in Vargmore, we had lunch at Shiloh's tavern, adorably called Stout & Spirit. I talked a while with Tryn's friends, but mostly with Riley, Sawyer's wife.

Riley was impossible to not like. She made me feel welcome and like we'd been friends for years already. She sometimes helped Shiloh with the bar, but her recent nausea from her pregnancy had her taking time off from work.

When I expressed that I had restaurant experience and had been training as a bartender, Shiloh jokingly informed me that I was hired. I almost said, "If you're serious, I will move here and start tomorrow."

Vargmore was everything Tryn said it would be when we first met. A hidden, close-knit community that was just as warm and friendly as it was dangerous and wild. All my yearning for a place to belong, a home that felt permanent and right, felt answered the moment we pulled up to Stout & Spirit. It almost felt like I had been in Vargmore before, had gone away for a while, and then finally returned.

I'd happily help out at that cheery little bar, and if the wolves needed medical attention, I could be an on-call vet. It felt so perfect. So right.

Every mile we passed on Tryn's motorcycle back to my little apartment felt like he was taking me *away* from home.

I tried to write it off as just missing what we'd had before, our undeniable connection before I knew about the lies. It was his home, and because I still wanted him, I wanted it to be *my* home.

Tryn pulled up to my place and to my surprise, killed the engine. I had been expecting him to drop me off.

"I'd like to talk some more, if you're up for it tonight," he said over his shoulder. "There's just more to explain."

Wasn't that the truth. He still hadn't told me why he really left in the middle of the night. Although I was starting to believe he wasn't married or attached to someone else. Everyone in Vargmore had treated me like, well, a new girlfriend meeting the extended circle of friends.

"Okay." I slid off the bike, away from the heat of his body, and headed for the front door.

Once we were inside, I felt my nerves start to creep up. Tryn looked nervous too. I could almost feel frazzled energy coming from him. He was about to drop something big. A bombshell.

"Do you want anything? Tea? Coffee?" I flitted around

the kitchen like a bird, turning on lights and opening cupboards, unable to sit still.

"No, thank you." Tryn just stood in my entryway, rubbing his hands together and scratching his beard.

"Should we, um," I gestured toward the living room, "sit down for this?"

"You can, if you'd like," he said. "I'd prefer to stand."

"Okay."

I headed for the couch and he trailed after until he was standing across from me. He still looked nervous as hell, eyes darted toward the window like he'd rather jump out of it than tell me whatever he needed to.

"Tryn," I prompted after a long minute of silence. "You're clearly nervous. It's making me nervous. So please, whatever it is, just get it out."

"Okay." He nodded, then said again, more to himself, "Okay." Finally, his eyes met mine. "So, you know how I told you the wolves in Vargmore are different?"

"Yeah." I nodded. "A rare subspecies, I'm assuming? Native only to that area?"

"Yes, that's correct." He took a deep inhale. "But that's not what makes them...different."

"Okay?"

He let the breath out in a huff, raking a hand back through his dark hair. "The vast majority of people in Vargmore *are* the wolves."

I narrowed my eyes, confused. "You mean the wolf population outnumbers the humans?"

"Yes, I mean, no. Not in the way you're thinking. Fuck, this is hard."

"Tryn, what are you trying to tell me?"

He huffed out another breath and said slowly, "The

people are the wolves, Emmaline." He touched a hand to his chest. "And the wolves are us."

I stared at him and blinked. *"What?"*

"We, the people native to Vargmore, have two forms. Human and wolf. We can change between the two."

He looked so serious, so desperate for me to believe him. And still, an uncomfortable laugh escaped my mouth. "Tryn, are you okay?"

"Yes! Look." He took his phone from his pocket and began scrolling. "You met Aria and Fallon, right?"

"Yeah, the two wolves."

He held out his phone for me to see. "This is also Fallon and Aria."

On his screen was a picture of an adorable couple sitting on a motorcycle. The woman sat behind the man, her arms hugging around his waist, her lips pressing a kiss to his cheek. The man was grinning, leaning his head back toward the woman, his hands covering hers on his stomach. They looked sweet, but I didn't recognize them. They weren't among the people in the tavern.

I looked at Tryn. "So you named the wolves after these people?"

"No," he sighed, putting his phone away. "I guess it's better if I just show you."

"Show me what?" My tone was exasperated. I didn't understand what he was trying to say at all. Surely not people actually turning into wolves, right?

"I have to take my clothes off for this." He pulled off his shirt and quickly began undoing his pants.

"Tryn!" I stood from the couch, unable to peel my eyes away from his bare skin despite how weirded out I was.

"Listen, I'm not in the mood. I don't want to do anything—"

"This isn't a sex thing, just watch. And…just remember." He paused, staring at me imploringly. "I would never, ever hurt you. This is going to be weird as fuck, but please don't be afraid. No matter what you see."

"Tryn, what the fuck is going on?" I kept my gaze on his face, even as he stripped his jeans off and stood completely naked in my living room.

He didn't answer, just took in another deep breath and closed his eyes.

Then, something started happening to his body.

"Oh my God!" My hands clapped over my mouth, eyes wide in horror as I watched.

Tryn's body was changing shape. His hands grew black claws, teeth growing long and sharp. His golden-brown eyes turned all the way to gold and became…something not human. Meanwhile, dark fur also sprouted all over his body and…was that a *tail* behind him?

Too much was happening at once. While he grew fur, teeth, and claws, the popping of bones and connective tissue filled the apartment. Tryn's shoulders popped from their sockets, the bones rolling freely under the skin. The same thing seemed to happen to his femurs from his pelvis and he fell forward.

"Oh God, Tryn!" I started forward, then stopped dead in my tracks. The shifting of bones looked so painful that I wanted to help, but I was also terrified. I'd never seen anything like this in my life. "Tryn, what's happening? What can I do?"

He seemed unable to speak, his nose and lips elongating into something like a snout. I reached for him but again, stopped frozen. I was caught between concern for the man I was falling for and abject terror. What the hell was this? And what could I do for this poor man on his hands and knees?

Wait, not hands and knees.

Paws. Four of them.

Large canine paws tipped with black claws.

It was quiet now, the migration of bones apparently finished.

I looked up from those paws into his face. A face that was not Tryn's but one I recognized instantly.

"Oh God..." I'd gone to the floor at some point and was now eye level with this creature in my living room. He was so big that he actually loomed over me. I fell back on my butt and scuttled backward until I hit the couch. "What the fuck?" I rubbed my eyes, wondering if I'd somehow ingested some LSD and was hallucinating this whole thing. "What the fuck? What the *fuck*?"

A massive wolf stared at me from across the living room. Not just any wolf, but *my* wolf. The one I hit with my car and who I'd released early. Who had come to my apartment one night.

The one wild animal I grew strangely attached to and missed terribly.

"It's you," I said in a disbelieving whisper.

With a soft whine, the wolf lowered his belly to the floor and rested his chin between his paws. He was just as beautiful and powerful as I remembered, if not more so now that he was no longer caged. And right then he looked harmless. Sweet, like he wanted hugs and ear scratches.

But again, what the actual fuck?

"You're...Tryn?" That very question felt like it broke my

brain. It was impossible. "You've been Tryn this whole time?"

The wolf let out a short bark and wagged his tail. Did that mean yes? Was Tryn still in there, conscious and aware?

"Can you, um, change back?" Could the wolf understand me? I felt like I was on another planet trying to communicate with an alien. "I would like to talk to Tryn."

The wolf pressed up, sitting on his haunches. His fur seemed to get sucked back into his hair follicles, and then came the sounds of bones and tissue rearranging themselves. I couldn't bring myself to look again, so I brought my forehead down on my knees.

After another minute, there was silence and then Tryn's soft voice. "It's me. I'm back."

I lifted my head to see him sitting cross-legged on the floor, his clothes in his lap to cover himself. His expression was apprehensive. Vulnerable.

I didn't know what to do or how to react to what I just saw. It was all I could do to keep from utterly losing my shit.

"What was that?" I asked as calmly as I could.

"That was my other form," Tryn said gently. "I can change between human and wolf."

"So," my breath shook as my mind raced, "that was *you* I hit with my car? You were the wolf we kept at the clinic?" It might have seemed obvious but my brain refused to connect the dots. Up until a minute ago, those dots simply weren't connectable.

"Yes," Tryn answered. "That was the real first time we met. Not when I came into the bar."

"Why *did* you come into Buck's Peak? Why were you… around here?"

Tryn dropped his gaze at my tone. I probably sounded accusatory, but I was really just trying my hardest to keep it together.

"Because I wanted to meet you as a man. I wanted to learn about you, get to know you. You had such a calming effect on my wolf that he was curious about you too. Seeing you was what kept my spirits up in that cage, so I just had to find out more about you."

The questions flew through my head too fast for me to catch up. "And everyone in Vargmore is…like you?"

"Not everyone, but the majority are."

"So every person I met in Stout & Spirit can turn into a wolf?"

"Shiloh can't," he said. "She's a witch, so she wields moon magic in a different way. But she doesn't have an animal inside her, so she can't change between forms."

"I'm sorry, moon magic?"

"Yeah." A tiny smile pulled at his lips for the first time since we got to my apartment. "Surprise, Dr. E. Magic is real."

"I…okay, wow." I rubbed at my forehead, trying to pick out another question from the alphabet soup of my brain. "And the reason you left in the middle of the night was because of," I gestured vaguely toward him, "this?"

Tryn cleared his throat, becoming serious again. "Right, yeah. A couple reasons. One was that the full moon was approaching in the next two days. When the full phase is that close, it has certain effects on my kind. Our animal instincts become more dominant. We become more, well, possessive of what's ours. We might snap at any perceived threats to our homes and families. And our, uh," he stroked his beard, "our sex drive and the urge to breed skyrockets."

"Oh." My face heated, and I remembered how insanely horny I was during that full moon night. Did his libido rub off on me or something?

"And when the moon is completely full," Tryn went on. "The shift is forced upon us. Any other time, we can change between human and wolf at will, and the two sides are more or less balanced. But on the full moon, we are fully wolf for one entire night." He swallowed thickly. "So I left because the shift also gets harder to control near the full moon, and I wasn't ready to explain the literal wolf in your bed, in case I shifted in my sleep." He went quiet, and then quickly muttered under his breath, "And also because I didn't want to bite you without you fully knowing what that entailed."

"Bite me?" I repeated.

"Not to hurt you," Tryn said quickly. "But to...claim you. As mine. So that no one else could say you were theirs. The urge to make a claiming bite is usually strongest during sex." He cringed. "I'm sorry. I know it sounds weird, but it's a wolf thing."

I remembered my own urge to bite him, the pressing need for it and the painful ache that he left. At the time, I was convinced the bite would feel like completion, it would enhance my orgasm and make everything *right*.

It had to be his wolf pheromones or something rubbing off on me, right? I had certainly never changed into a wolf on the full moon before.

"What are you thinking?" Tryn asked after a while of silence.

"I don't know. A million things." I propped my elbow

on my knee and rested my head in my hand. "Mostly, how is this possible? How come nobody else knows about this?"

"Because we keep it that way," Tryn said in a low growl. "Most of us don't venture out of our world, and humans rarely stumble into ours."

"So why did you?"

He opened his mouth like he was going to say something, then promptly shut it. "Dunno. I was feeling reckless, I guess," he muttered.

Funny. I thought my choosing to date him was reckless. Straight-laced, studious Emmaline with a long-haired, muscular biker. Turns out, I didn't even know the half of what I was getting into.

"So, what now?" I asked.

Tryn pulled in a deep lungful of air. "That depends on how you're feeling about all this. I would still like to, you know, see where this goes. But that's contingent on you being okay with what I am."

He still wanted us to see each other? Could I really date a man who was also a wolf? I guess that was what I'd been doing all along, but knowingly?

I heaved out a sigh. "I...don't know, Tryn. This has really fucked what I thought I knew about the world. I feel like I don't know anything anymore."

A small, forced laugh left his mouth. "Yeah, I know it's a lot. But I couldn't keep this part of myself hidden from you anymore. It killed me to lie to you. I just...I like you too much."

He gave me a hopeful look as if waiting for me to return the sentiment. As much as I wanted to reassure him that my feelings hadn't changed, and they truthfully hadn't, I was beyond overwhelmed by what he showed me and needed to process it all.

"I'm not saying no," I told him. "I just need time to think about all this."

His smile was gentle, reassuring, but the slight droop in his shoulders made my chest ache. "Of course. I understand." He unfolded his shirt in his lap and pushed his arms through the sleeves. "I'll get dressed and get out of your hair."

I stood and at the last second, turned my back to give him privacy. I had already seen him naked, but it didn't feel proper now.

The room became filled with an awkward silence, only the rustling of Tryn's clothes making any sound. Was it only a few days ago that I wanted to get those pants off myself? That we were in bed together and it felt so natural and right?

Now? We felt like strangers.

"I'm decent," Tryn said. When I turned to face him, his expression was grave. "It probably goes without saying, but I will anyway. Don't tell anyone what you saw here. I don't believe you'd lead anyone to Vargmore, but no one from this world will find it even if you try."

"Of course, I won't," I said with a fervent shake of my head. "I would never."

He gave me a curt nod and started for the door. I hated this distance between us, even if I was the one who put it there.

"Tryn, I—I'll, um..."

He stopped with his hand on the knob but didn't turn around.

"I'll call you. Soon," I offered lamely. It wasn't lost on

me that I used the same non-committal phrase he'd given me when he left my bed.

The smile he gave over his shoulder, his eyes not meeting mine, was strained, like he didn't believe me. "Okay," he said flatly. "Bye, Emmaline."

And then, he left.

CHAPTER 18

TRYN

Stupid. Fucking. Idiot.

It was too soon. I shouldn't have tried to tell her everything in the same day. Poor Emmaline had been too overwhelmed already. And after seeing a man turn into a wolf, she probably thought she was going crazy.

Fucking dumbass. I'd been too impatient, too eager to come clean without thinking the ramifications all the way through. She was human, for moon's sake.

And now I'd fucked up everything.

The odds of Emmaline still wanting to be together was the longest of long shots. My world, the very person I was, had never existed to her until last night. I was too strange for her. We were literally from two different worlds. How could we possibly make it work?

Staring at my bedroom ceiling, my hand curled in the center of my chest. My fingers dug into my own skin until it hurt. I could see the silver fate thread in my periphery, that infernal rope tying me to her, and wanted to rip it from my chest.

What was the point? All I did was disrupt her life, lie to her, hurt her, and weird her the fuck out. If I hadn't been able to see the damn thread, I never would have met her. She would have been better off.

Fuck this so-called gift. This curse.

"Are you happy? You've had your fun." The moon was millions of miles away, a cold rock in space. But I knew Her magic, knew She could hear me. "I hope it was amusing for you, watching me fall for someone I could never have. But I'm over it. Take this away. I don't want it anymore."

My hand cut across the silver thread. It stayed intact, like my hand had passed through a beam of light. And to my complete lack of surprise, the moon didn't answer my request.

I heard Gran's voice in my head instead. "It's not our job to understand the moon. To manipulate Her into performing our whims. She sees all and loves us as a mother does. Sometimes that entails tough love and lessons to be learned." It was something she told me as a pup a long time ago, when I asked why my parents had to be taken away from me.

My hand dropped to the bed with a heavy sigh. Before I could give much thought to what the lesson was with Emmaline, a heavy pounding came to my door.

"Pack meeting," Ruse barked through the wood before moving on to the next door.

I rolled up with a groan and headed down to the main floor of the lodge. Pack business would keep my mind off of Emmaline, at least.

While coming down the stairs, I halted a step at the sight of Camael, leader of the angels standing in the open dining hall in the lodge. His navy blue suit was crisp, not a wrinkle or piece of lint to be seen. The angel's brilliant white wings were tense, drawn in close to his back. His arms mirrored the same tension, crossed over his chest. Likewise, his expression was tight-lipped and eyebrows drawn down.

Sawyer and Derric always joked that the angels' halos must have been shoved up their asses, because their faces always looked like they had some kind of obstruction in that area. Right then, Camael's anal-halo seemed especially bothersome.

He was joined by three other angels, two males I didn't know and a female I recognized as his sister, Laylah.

Laylah was classically beautiful with red hair, green eyes, and a pleasing symmetry to her face. But it wasn't her looks that stopped me for a second time on my way down the stairs.

"Fuck." I rubbed my eyes and looked again, then swore a second time. My curse was again showing me what others couldn't see.

In faint outlines superimposed over her body like tracing paper, I saw puncture marks on Laylah's neck and blood dripping down her throat. She turned her head to speak to one of the other angels and the opposite side of her neck showed more of the same, puncture marks and blood.

I gripped the banister hard enough for my knuckles to turn white and couldn't stop staring. Most of the time, I only saw threads. Threads based on fate, truth, and in shifters, a thread connecting their two forms. Other times, I had visions like these. Right then, my curse was showing me clear signs of a vampire feeding off of the angel.

But when? How? The angels were especially protective

of their females, almost archaically so, and they *never* associated with vampires.

Even more strange, I saw a thread stretching out from Laylah's back, right between her wings. It shimmered red and gold, twinkling like a dew-covered spider's web as it went through the lodge's front door, stretching from east to west. The only territory strictly in that direction was Sanguine.

My eyes narrowed. Could an angel truly have a vampire for a fated mate? Was such a thing even possible?

"Tryn." Derric's voice pulled me from my swirling confusion and my gaze jerked to him. "Join us whenever you're ready." The Alpha's tone had a bite of irritation, and I hurried the rest of the way to join my pack.

Once we were gathered around Derric's high-backed chair at the far side of the room, the Alpha took his seat, and with it, control of the floor. "As always, Howling Death appreciates a visit from our winged neighbors to the north. What can we do for you, Camael?"

Derric's words were hospitable, but his tone and expression were more along the lines of, "What the fuck do you want this time, assholes?"

Camael stepped forward, not sparing a glance at the hungry-eyed werewolves surrounding him on either side. "Vampires have once again been spotted on the streets of my territory. I've come to find out why our...dear neighbors to the south," he said with a sneer, "have not done a thing for the protection of both of our territories. Surely, you must know that these vermin will find their way to Vargmore if they are allowed to infiltrate Helios City."

"We investigated the last incident and came up with no evidence of vampires. That was just over a week ago, if you'll recall. The so-called witnesses in your territory were entirely unhelpful. So a better question might be, why don't you put your shiny shoes on the ground for once and investigate what's going on in your own city?"

Camael bristled at the thinly-veiled insult. "We have reason to believe the vampires are crossing into our territory from yours. This affects both of us, Derric."

The Alpha shifted his eyes to Orson. "Seen any suspicious activity at the borders?"

"No, Alpha," the wolf replied coolly. His icy gaze leveled on the angel. "I have motion-activated cameras set along our entire perimeter. We have regular patrols around the whole territory and follow-up with any unfamiliar scents. Not to mention our barrier of magic that is regularly reinforced by our witches. If so much as a blade of grass twitches anywhere on the border, I know about it."

I knew all about our security measures, but it was still impressive to hear. Orson had made sure our border was ironclad ever since that rogue dragon shifter had snuck in and threatened Shiloh a few months ago.

Camael shook his head. "I have no doubts as to your abilities, but they must be bypassing you somehow. Our perimeter is also guarded at every point, with magically enforced barriers. They are not coming directly from Sanguine to Helios."

"Well, they're not coming through us." Derric shrugged. "Maybe you have a blind spot."

"We don't," the angel hissed. "My kind can fucking fly, in case you forgot. My perimeter is regularly checked from the sky. We've missed nothing. You wolves, on the other hand, must have your noses so close to the ground that you've missed what's going on right above your heads."

Derric stood from his chair with a low growl, teeth bared. "You want to keep talking about how your species is superior to mine, in *my* home? Come on, angel. Get it all off your chest."

Several people moved in, but I was the fastest, bringing my open palm against Derric's sternum. "Easy, Alpha. This overgrown chicken isn't worth it."

Laylah had stepped in front of her brother, her hands against his shoulders. Camael towered over her, looking easily able to push past her slight weight, but Laylah held him firm.

"Take a breath, brother," she murmured to him. "Please. These people are our allies. We are guests in their territory." Her eyes flicked up to him. "You should apologize."

Camael scoffed like that was the last thing he would do, but his sister's words must have reached the rational part of his brain. He took a step back, straightening the lapels of his suit jacket.

"Forgive me, Alpha. The idea that these creatures may be feeding on my people is...very upsetting. My emotions got the better of me."

There was a beat of silence as we all waited for an 'I apologize', but it seemed the leading angel had too much pride for that. I glanced at Laylah, who still had metaphysical puncture marks and blood on her neck.

"The harm caused by vampires is something my kind knows well," Derric said tightly, his heart still pounding against my palm. "Many of my pack standing here now have lost parents and grandparents to their bloodlust. Myself included." He finally stepped back, but continued to eye Camael warily. "Believe me when I say I would never wish a vampire attack on anyone. And that my pack will do everything in our power to prevent a repeat of what happened to us."

"Then why won't you help us?" Camael bit out.

"We have." Derric resettled into his chair. "And we will be happy to continue offering our support. But you coming in here and accusing our security measures of being flawed is not the way to nurture our alliance."

Camael's wings drooped an almost imperceptible distance in the barest sign of humility. "That was not my intention, Alpha. This matter just feels extremely urgent and from my view, our allies are in no hurry to help."

"Respectfully, what more can we do?" Derric opened his palms. "Last week, we lent you our tracking abilities, our noses and ears, our time and energy, to no avail. Do you have anything to go on besides some unreliable witnesses?"

The angel clenched his teeth. "I just *know* they've been within my borders. Those witnesses wouldn't make such claims for no reason."

Derric tried his best to give a sympathetic look. "We can't prioritize your territory over our own without more evidence. I'm sorry."

All the werewolves in the room held a collective breath, waiting for the angel to throw another tantrum, but Camael only sighed. His wings sank lower in defeat. "I understand. I appreciate you hearing me anyway, Alpha. When I contact you again, it will be with more substantial proof."

He turned to leave, his brethren falling in step behind him. Laylah was the last to follow. She gave a tight smile and small nod of her head to Derric, who returned the gesture.

Once the angels left, the atmosphere in the lodge

immediately relaxed. Wolves murmured to each other, while I rubbed my forehead. Seeing a high-ranking angel like Laylah covered in blood was not a good sign, and it wasn't one I would forget easily.

"What do we think?" Derric asked the room, inviting anyone to give their thoughts. "Are vampires sneaking into Helios City?"

"I'm sure Camael believes that," Ruse scoffed. "But is it actually happening? No. He's losing it. Flying too damn close to the sun or whatever."

"Or his so-called witnesses are," someone else piped up. "On some kind of angel street drug, maybe?"

"Can angels even do drugs?" another wolf wondered.

"Whatever's going on, if anything, it's not our business at this point." Ruse shrugged.

"Fair point, but here's a question." Sawyer stepped into the open area in the middle of the room. "At what point do we get involved? By the time a vampire kidnaps an angel victim to feed on, it might be too late."

All the murmuring fell silent. Everyone knew he was thinking of his own mate, Riley, who had been a vampire's blood pet for over a year. She had been fed on for so long and lost so much blood, she almost didn't make it.

"I'll encourage Camael to keep in touch with me about any developments," Derric said, looking earnestly at Sawyer. "We'll do everything we can to prevent it from getting to that point." His jaw set in a hard line. "I will not make the same mistake again, Enforcer."

Sawyer jerked his chin down in a nod, seemingly satis-fied with that answer.

"Waste of effort if you ask me," Ruse muttered. "Angels, you know. Everything's gotta be dramatic with them."

"Camael's not being dramatic," I bit out. "There *is* something going on between vampires and angels."

The Alpha narrowed his shrewd gaze on me. "Did you see something?"

I told him about the puncture marks and blood I saw on Laylah, and everyone's face paled. As for the red-gold fate thread running from her to the vampire territory, I kept that to myself. If she truly was destined to be with a vampire, there was nothing I, my pack, nor the angels, could do to sway fate.

"Fuck." Sawyer rubbed his jaw. "Do we tell Camael?"

"That's risky," Ruse said. "He'll lock her up like a prisoner." The VP focused on me. "Could it be a warning?"

"I truly don't know."

My visions changed based on circumstances, and sometimes they were more symbolic than literal in nature. For example, I always used to see a type of shield around Sawyer and interpreted it as him guarding his heart. Until Riley, he never let anyone emotionally closer to him than a friend. Once she came around, his shield started falling away. His fated mate had gotten past his armor to the heart of him.

In any case, my visions always came true in one way or another. And what I saw on Laylah looked pretty fucking literal.

"The plan stays the same for now," Derric announced. "I'll touch base regularly with Camael, and if anything more concrete turns up, we'll go from there." He lifted a hand from his armrest, effectively dismissing us. "That's all. Keep your noses and ears sharp on your perimeter patrols."

The crowd of werewolves dispersed, some shifting

immediately as they headed outside, others retiring to various rooms.

"Hey, Tryn." Sawyer caught up to me and grabbed my shoulder in a friendly squeeze. "When's your mate coming back? Riley's been asking. She wants to gush over some book series they're apparently both reading."

Well, fuck. So much for being effectively distracted.

Sawyer must have noticed some change in me, because he narrowed his eyes in confusion and didn't let go of my shoulder. "Shit, Tryn. What happened?"

I removed his hand from my shoulder and started up the stairs. "Something I should have seen coming."

CHAPTER 19

EMMALINE

A s someone who usually made decisions without anyone else's input, I found it really, really diffi- cult to not talk to anyone about what Tryn had told me. What he'd *shown* me.

I thought about talking to Annika or Joey, but my head was so messed up, I was terrified of saying too much and potentially exposing Tryn.

God, I saw him turning into that wolf, *my* wolf, every time I closed my eyes.

After the initial shock wore off, I became less weirded out every time I pictured it. And wasn't *that* weird, that it was becoming less weird to me?

He was still a man. That was the conclusion I kept returning to. A tall, gorgeous man who was funny, warm, sweet, and an incredible kisser. A man with secrets, yes. Secrets that he did tell me, at the risk of his home and safety of his people. Was it really so bad or strange that he could turn into a wolf?

The ache of missing him never left. The sense of wrongness caused by his absence was my constant companion. As time went on, the ache only grew worse.

I felt desperate to talk to someone but would never betray my promise to Tryn. No one could know about Vargmore or what he was.

Except for the people who already lived there.

An idea wiggled into my brain and wouldn't leave. I paced on it, wearing a path down in my apartment, then walking the trail around my complex. The idea took root in my head until my fingers itched for my car keys, ready to take action.

What if I just went to Vargmore myself and talked to Riley? She had said she was from Arizona, so she must have gone through something similar with Sawyer.

The thought of going back there myself made my stomach clench in knots, but I needed a sounding board. Someone to listen to everything going on in my mind, and who better than my new friend who knew exactly where I was coming from?

Hell, if I could find my way to Stout & Spirit, Shiloh would probably be a great listening ear too.

My keys were in my hand, locking the door behind me before I realized I'd arrived at a decision. Within minutes, I was on the stretch of highway that Tryn had taken me on his motorcycle just two days before.

I had a pretty good sense of direction, and while I didn't *exactly* remember the off-beaten path Tryn had taken, I was confident I could remember the general area.

Well over an hour later, I was nearly tearing my hair out in frustration. Where the fuck was it?

I merged onto the freeway from the on-ramp for the third time, driving way under the speed limit to closely inspect the trees and brush alongside the road. Good thing there was little traffic way out here in the sticks.

Hugging the shoulder, I searched for that narrow, unmarked gravel road that could fit a single motorcycle or small car. The sun was going down fast, so it needed to appear to me soon or else I'd never be able to see it.

"Come on, come on," I muttered. "Show yourself."

A blue sports car came up fast behind me and the driver laid on their horn, clearly disapproving of my grandma highway speed, before swerving around to pass me. I ignored them, but their obnoxious LED headlights picked up something ahead that caught my eye. I pulled up to that spot and a surge of victory lifted my spirits.

Tall grasses and shrubs shielded most of the hidden road from view, but this had to be it. I flipped on my headlights and turned off the highway, heading through the forest to another world.

"I should've bought a Jeep," I muttered as my car bounced and jerked on the uneven terrain. "Or a motorcycle."

The trees blocked out most of the sunlight, and when night fell after about another hour of driving, the darkness was on another level. Unlike that night I accidentally hit Tryn, where my headlights illuminated the whole road, this darkness seemed to swallow up the weak little lights from my car.

It was then that I realized that maybe driving by myself to a hidden world where werewolves, witches, and probably other supernatural beings existed, probably wasn't the best idea.

Tryn and I had reached Stout & Spirit after about an

hour of driving on this road, but the cozy little tavern was nowhere in sight. Had I missed a turn somewhere?

I gripped the steering wheel, leaning close to the windshield to peer into the darkness. Turning around kept crossing my mind, but I didn't want to end up more lost than I already was. If I kept going, I'd have to end up somewhere in Vargmore, right? If not, I'd still be in the sticks of northern California. Probably still in Plumas County.

I drove on, watching the road with the meager illumination thrown out by my headlights. It was the same narrow gravel path, so it had to lead somewhere.

Some time later, the gravel became a paved road, smoother and more refined. My tires almost seemed to sigh in merciful relief. I didn't remember a paved road leading to Stout & Spirit, but I hadn't exactly been thinking about it at the time.

The trees and brush started to thin out, revealing bright stars in the night sky. I couldn't see the moon yet but for some reason, knowing it was out there, watching over all, gave me a sense of comfort.

The road wasn't just paved at this point, it was pristine. Smooth and black as oil, like the asphalt had just been poured. Once the trees finally gave way to a clearing, I had to stop. My foot stomped on the brake, making the tires squeal as I stared in open-mouthed shock.

Those lights in the sky hadn't been from stars but from buildings. Fucking skyscrapers. I was staring at what looked like the financial district of a major city.

An actual fucking city, rivaling the likes of San Francisco or Los Angeles. Out here. In the middle of nowhere.

But how?

The city closest to Fulsburg was probably Reno, and

even that place was small potatoes compared to this. This place was a fucking metropolis. There was no way it could be kept hidden in the middle of nowhere.

Unless...

Unless it was hidden in the same way that Vargmore was.

I didn't know how long I sat there, car idling in the middle of an empty road, staring at the skyscrapers, knuckles white on the steering wheel. Eventually, I lifted my foot from the brake and tapped gently on the gas, nudging the car forward. Questions flooded my mind as I approached the city like an ant to a sleeping giant.

How much of Tryn's world was there, really? Was this the only city or were there more? Did these people know about werewolves? Where did Vargmore fit into the bigger picture, and how big was that picture? Were there enough fantastical people and places to fit a country, or even a planet, if you only knew where to look?

My entire perception of the world, existence, reason, and logic had been completely blown apart. And yet I could not stop inching forward to find out more.

There was a small turn-out area next to the road just on the outskirts of the city, and I decided to park there and keep going on foot. Being a pedestrian was pretty universal, but I didn't know if this place had weird traffic laws or speed limits. The last thing I wanted to do was get in trouble, or an accident, because I didn't know the laws.

I followed the road into the glittering city center. The skyscrapers stretched above me so high, I had to crane my neck to follow the lines.

And that was when I bumped into someone for the first time.

"Oh shit, I'm sorry!"

"Watch it, human," came the disdainful sneer of the person I'd bumped into.

I spun on the sidewalk, watching the tall, ethereal beauty walk off. It was a woman with a set of massive wings on her back. She wore a backless evening gown and those wings definitely looked like they were part of her anatomy, not a piece of some cheesy costume. They were covered in black feathers with a gold and purple iridescent sheen.

At a crosswalk, the woman lifted the hem of her elegant dress a few inches and bent her knees deeply. Then with a single, powerful beat of those wings, she was in the air.

She was flying. With wings. *Her* wings. She was a woman who had wings and used them to fly.

Holy fucking shit. Was she an angel?

A rude angel, to be fair. But a winged person nonetheless.

I watched her fly, her form growing smaller as she glided elegantly alongside one of the skyscrapers. When she was almost too far up to see anymore, I saw her land on a balcony where other people were gathered. Other people with wings of all sorts of colors.

My gaze moved away from the balcony party across the skyline, and only then did it hit me that this city was *full* of winged people.

Some were in mid-flight, while others walked the streets like normal pedestrians. At an outdoor patio across the street, two men sat at a table over what looked like coffee and pastries. They sat in backless chairs, basically wide stools with more support, their wings angled in a way so they wouldn't run into each other. One man's wings were a creamy white color with a silvery sheen catching the light. The other's had black feathers with golden-purple highlights, much like the woman I'd bumped into.

A sleek, shiny motorcycle rumbled past me, and its rider had wings as well. Come to think of it, most of the vehicles on the smooth, dark roads were motorcycles. Cars probably weren't too comfortable if you had to cram your wings inside.

These people have wings, holy shit! My mind couldn't get over that fact, and I couldn't stop gawking at all of them. It didn't help that they all looked inhumanly beautiful as well.

There were non-winged people as well, but they were by far the minority. I counted maybe one normal-looking human walking down the street to every five angels.

If the humans saw any kinship in me, felt any desire to help one of their own who was clearly lost and awestruck, they didn't show it. Everyone was coming and going in a hurry, their faces looking down at a cellphone screen or straight ahead with single-minded purpose.

At some point, I'd have to talk to someone, ask for directions to Stout & Spirit, but my mind was too overloaded with new information. Beautiful people with wings. People who could fly. A huge, bustling city apparently hidden in the middle of nowhere. Full of people with fucking *wings*!

Slowly, the lights of the city seemed to fade, and for the first time, I actively checked my surroundings and muttered a curse. I'd been so busy gawking at the city and its winged residents that I didn't realize I had stumbled onto a much darker, more run-down street.

This part of the city was definitely older, with aged bricked buildings rather than the shiny glass and steel structures in the central area. Huge cracks and potholes filled the streets, unlike the pristine asphalt that I'd walked on moments ago. Faded graffiti covered the crumbling brick walls and dumpsters lined narrow alleyways. The lights here were dim and cast a sickly yellow glow, throwing long ominous shadows on the narrow streets.

Even cities full of angels had their slums, apparently.

A creaking sound put me on high alert and I froze in place, watching a door open in the alley just ahead. A man with no wings stepped out, allowing the door to close behind him.

He leaned against the building, the yellow exterior light carving around his silhouette. I could only make out general shapes but saw that he was tall with a mess of spiky hair. He propped one foot on the wall behind him and proceeded to light a cigarette. The small flame showed a sharp, angular face with prominent cheekbones. Dark hair fell over his forehead and a tattoo decorated his throat. He wasn't unattractive, but there was a dark, mean look to him.

Was this guy a werewolf? Tryn could be intimidating, but this man was scary in a completely different way.

Something was off about the cigarette too. The end glowed red like normal, but the smoke he exhaled on a sigh was also red. An odd smell drifted over in the air, something earthy and metallic.

By the time my rational brain caught up with all my observations and figured out that I probably shouldn't catch this man's attention, his head had turned lazily in my direction.

"Can I help you?" he asked in a bored drawl.

"Um, no. No, I'm good, thank you." I fully knew that I

should turn around and walk away, but there was something enthralling about this man. I was equal parts fascinated and scared out of my mind.

"A likely story." He flicked his cigarette, sending sparks and red ash to the filthy ground before taking another drag. "You lost, little human?"

"No! No, I'm good. Just...walking."

He turned his whole body toward me then and took a few steps closer. All my instincts screamed with fear, but I could not seem to bring myself to move.

The light showed more of his face now, deepening the shadows under his brow and cheekbones to make him look even more sinister. And his irises...were they red?

"You smell an awful lot like a werewolf for a human," he noted casually. The corner of his mouth ticked up like that amused him. "Like to roll around with the furballs, do you?"

"I'm...dating a werewolf." The fact that I uttered that sentence aloud to a red-eyed stranger in a seedy alley in a strange city full of winged beings felt like the least bizarre thing that had happened to me lately.

"Dating?" The man laughed, then coughed, red smoke coming out of his mouth and nostrils. "You're so painfully human, it's adorable. Wolves don't date. If one's sniffing after you, he's convinced you're his mate for life. Although..." His red gaze fell to my neck and his pupils seemed to dilate at the sight of my pulse. "No mating bite, which is interesting."

Something clicked inside me when he said *mate*. I didn't fully understand but some instinct told me that was the right word. Tryn was my mate, and that meant no one else could touch me.

Feeling emboldened by this knowledge, I crossed my arms and finally managed to step back. "We haven't reached that point yet, but yes, I do have a mate. Now, do you know how to get to Stout & Spirit?"

"Stout & Spirit?" The man laughed again, his canine teeth looking particularly long and sharp. "You're a long way from Vargmore, little human."

"But...you know how to get there?" I didn't know whether to feel disappointed or hopeful. At least I hadn't stumbled into a world completely different from Tryn's.

"I do. And because I'm such a nice guy, I wouldn't even be opposed to taking you there."

He was just as much a nice guy as scorpions were cuddly.

"No, thank you." I backed away more insistently now, eager to come out of the shadows. "I'll find another way. Have a nice night."

"Who's your mate?" The guy tossed the butt of his spent cigarette and went back to leaning against the wall. He seemed in no hurry to follow me out of the alley.

"Tryn," I answered without thinking.

The man's gaze snapped to mine, red eyes bright and alert. Then he moved at such blinding speed, pulling up right in front of me.

"You're mated to a Howling Death wolf?" he asked in an awed whisper.

"I..." A memory came up of Tryn's broad back, right before I embraced him on the motorcycle. The leather vest he wore with a large patch of a wolf's skull on the back, jaws open wide.

"...Yes," I said in a daze, like the answer was being forcefully pulled from my throat.

"Fascinating," came the raspy drawl.

The moment I tried to look at the man again, his hand passed in front of my face. My vision went dark and my knees buckled like a puppet's strings that had been cut.

"Easy, now." The man caught me before I hit the ground, sliding an arm behind my knees and my back.

Fear and alarm rang through me, but I couldn't move or make a sound. The red-eyed man carried me like a bride, my head resting on a leanly muscled shoulder. His touch was revolting to me, but I couldn't do a damn thing. And then my consciousness started to fade like I'd been drugged.

"Let's get you home to your mate, little human," the man said cheerfully as I clung to wakefulness with all my strength. "And if everything goes well, I won't even have to hurt you."

CHAPTER 20

TRYN

Drowning one's sorrows was such a cliche. But I suppose cliches exist for a reason.

"I'm cutting you off after this one." Shiloh gave me the stink eye as she placed another beer in front of me.

"Don't worry. I'm not gonna shift and piss on something," I told her. "Or *not* shift and piss. I guess that would be worse."

"Shifted or not, I *will* swat you on the nose with a rolled-up magazine if you do." Despite the threat, her glare softened. "I hate seeing you like this, Tryn."

"Thanks. I hate feeling like this, but what can you do?"

Shiloh's hand floated up to her neck, where the two crescent-shaped scars of Orson's teeth marked her as his mate. His one and only partner for life.

"Don't give up on her so fast," the witch said softly. "After everything Orson and I went through before officially mating, I firmly believe the moon likes to test us, you know?

Throw a bunch of obstacles our way, see what our relationships are really made of. You have to fight for it, Tryn."

"It's not so much an obstacle as it is a fundamental incompatibility," I argued. As much as it hurt, it was true. Fate was just playing a game with me.

"You said she asked to be bitten, right?" Shiloh pressed. "That has to mean something."

"I don't believe it does."

After talking to Shiloh and Aria, I found out both had the urge to bite and be bitten when getting newly intimate with their mates. However, Shiloh was not a latent wolf, and Aria was. So it didn't necessarily mean that Emmaline was of my kind.

For all I knew, the biting just signaled strong sexual attraction and nothing else.

"Emmaline's not like other humans," Shiloh insisted. "Aria and Riley both said as much."

I shrugged. "Doesn't mean she wants to live among a bunch of shapeshifters and moon magic wielders."

"It's not like she ran away screaming. You said she asked for time, you brickhead."

"Because she has the decency to be polite."

Shiloh sighed and flicked a rag over her shoulder. "You're impossible."

"All the better that she doesn't end up with me."

"You're allowed to be sad, Tryn. But this mopey, whimpering-into-my-beer thing isn't you."

"I'm not whimpering."

The front door creaked open before Shiloh could go at me again, and nails clicked over the hardwood floors. I turned to see Orson's silver-white wolf dash into the tavern, a dark bundle in his jaws. He darted behind the bar and shifted into a naked man breathing hard and covered in sweat.

"Babe, are you okay?" Shiloh put a hand on her mate's back as he bent over to unwrap the bundle he'd been carrying. "Did you run across the whole territory?"

"Emmaline's in trouble," Orson panted. The bundle turned out to be his phone rolled up into a pair of sweatpants, which he promptly started swiping on. His glare at me was pure ice. "Way to answer my fucking calls, by the way."

"Trouble how? Where is she?" I couldn't dwell on the fact that I'd taken a page out of Emmaline's book and left my phone at the lodge so that I wouldn't be tempted to call her.

"Northwestern border. My perimeter camera picked this up." Orson turned his phone screen to face me, and the image made my heart stop.

Thorne, leader of the vampires with a charming little outfit called Blood 'til Dawn MC, rulers of the Sanguine territory, stood with what looked like an unconscious woman cradled against his chest. He held her with one arm, while the other extended out to show a message written in some dark substance on the inside of his forearm.

It read, *TRYN. COME ALONE.*

"I swung by the lodge while looking for you, so the pack already knows. We're riding out to back you up—"

I cut off Orson with a rough scrape of my barstool against the floor. "Call them off," I snarled. White-hot rage sobered me in an instant. My wolf clawed to come out, to rip into that soulless bloodsucking insect until he was in pieces, and I was moments away from letting him.

"Do *not* go up against that vampire alone!" Orson called after me. "Thorne wants something; it's a fucking trap."

"You think I care? He has my mate! No one is getting between my teeth and his throat."

Orson's protests died off in the distance, becoming meaningless background noise as I tore my clothes off. The next thing I knew, I was sprinting on all fours, heading straight for the northwestern border.

If that was her blood on his arm...If that vampire had cut her, fucking *bitten* her to send a message to me, I was going to kill him. It didn't matter if he killed me first, I'd come back as a vengeful ghost and haunt that sick fucker until he walked into the sunlight to be rid of me.

That was all I could think of as I raced across the territory. That and a desperate prayer up to the moon that I wasn't too late for Emmaline.

))))) ● ● (((((

THORNE WAS RIGHT where Orson said he'd be, standing on the vampire side of the magical barrier that separated our territories, an unmoving Emmaline in his arms. The last thing I wanted to do was talk to the scum like he was a person, but I had to make sure my mate was okay.

I shifted to my human form, ignoring the quirked eyebrow and mild look of approval on Thorne's face. "Nice cock, werewolf. No wonder this little human went wandering in search of you."

"What did you do to her?" My wolf simmered just under my skin, punctuating every word with a growl.

"Relax, she's fine. Just put her to sleep, after compelling some *very* interesting information out of her."

"Did you bite her?" I didn't give a fuck what he compelled Emmaline to say. If he gave her so much as a papercut, I'd unleash all the fury of my wolf on him.

Thorne gave me a bored look. "I don't actually prefer the taste of humans. I will say it was tempting to get a rise out of you, but you can lower your hackles. All of her blood is safely inside her body."

"Then give her to me." I extended my arm out across the barrier, the prickle of magic making my skin itch. "Hand over my mate and I'll tell my pack there was no issue here. You can carry on skulking in the dark like you always do."

The vampire didn't bring her any closer. He actually backed up a step, turning his body and Emmaline away from me, and flashed a grin full of fangs when I growled.

"I will be happy to hand over your mate, werewolf, but I need more from you than that."

"Name it," I snarled. "And do it quickly, before I lose patience and tear out your throat."

"I want you to look away from the rumors of my kind being seen in Helios City," Thorne said. "If you smell or see one of us on those streets, no you didn't. If Camael recruits you for K-9 duty, you'll find no traces of us. As far as Howling Death is concerned, the reports of vampires in the angel's city are completely unsubstantiated. Am I clear, werewolf?"

The ramifications of what he was asking hit me with a cold dose of clarity, cutting through the heat of my aggression. For one, it wasn't my decision to make, it was Derric's. But what floored me was this creature, a centuries-long enemy, was asking me to side with him. To betray an ally for *his* benefit.

I shook my head, a mirthless laugh of disbelief escaping my lips. "You have the biggest, brassiest balls of any vampire I've ever met, to ask such a thing of *me*."

Thorne wasn't smiling anymore. He stared at me with those creepy red eyes, the waning moon reflecting silver in his pupils. "I want your word, werewolf. Now, under the moon. And I'll hand over your mate, safe and sound."

"What are you even doing in Helios City?" I asked him. Not that I cared, but the notion was just absurd. Angels used sunlight to power everything. Vampires couldn't stand daylight unless they were hopped up on a drug called Draitrium, which Thorne supposedly didn't condone. So what kind of business would he have there?

"Not your concern," the vampire said. "No one is getting hurt. You don't need to know anything beyond that."

"Bullshit. How are you even getting into the city?"

"Not through your territory, don't worry," he sneered. "I don't enjoy stepping in dog shit while crossing borders."

"I'm not the Alpha," I said. "Even if I wanted to say yes to such an insane fucking demand, I can't make that decision."

"You can and just not tell your pack." Thorne shifted Emmaline in his arms and her head lolled on the top of her spine. "Or I can drain your mate faster than you can blink."

"You're dead if your fangs touch her." I let my wolf rise, the shift effortless with our combined protective instincts over Emmaline.

I dropped to all fours and approached Throne, my ears flattened and all my sharp teeth on display. The barrier's magic floated over me, a signal that I had left my territory and entered his.

Like I cared. He could run straight to hell itself and I'd still go after him to get my mate back.

Thorne backed up a few steps and I followed, snarling. Vampires had incredible speed over short distances, but even if I lost him temporarily, I could track his scent and Emmaline's. Would he run like a coward, though? Even bottom feeders like vampires had to have some pride.

To my surprise, Thorne began lowering himself to the ground. His eyes remained fixed on me as he dropped a knee and began to gently lay Emmaline on the forest floor. Her eyes were still closed, her body slack, but her brow pinched in a frown as Throne removed his hands from her.

I hated that he had touched her at all and darted forward with a whine to check on her. Her breaths seemed normal, and I smelled nothing suspicious on her mouth or skin. She stirred under the frantic contact of my cold, wet nose dragging all over her. When she moaned a little, a sign that she was waking up, I couldn't help myself from taking small affectionate licks of her face.

"Tryn?" she mumbled woozily, hands reaching for me.

Before she could touch me, something barreled into me with the force of a car and sent me rolling and tumbling away.

I coughed and wheezed as I finally came to a stop, struggling for a breath as I got back to all fours. Fuck, how had I been so short-sighted? Of course Thorne would seek to lower my defenses and use my mate as a distraction.

A scream wrenched me around, and the sight before me would have me seeing red for years to come.

Thorne had Emmaline's hair in his fist, pulling her head

back to expose her throat. She scratched and tore at his other arm braced across her torso, her legs scrambling for purchase in the dirt.

The fucking vampire had the balls to make eye contact with me and and smirk as he lowered his fangs to my mate's neck.

That was as close as he got. I ran at him with speed I didn't know I was capable of. He let go of Emmaline at the last second, giving me an opening to crash into him like a battering ram. We collided with enough impact to send us rolling, and I closed my jaws on whatever I could reach, making sure to drag him with me and away from her.

We fought like hell, rolling and tumbling, trying to grab, punch, kick, bite, anything to get the upper hand. Bitter blood filled my mouth and fabric ripped.

When Thorne's weight suddenly lifted away, I rolled to my paws, intent on chasing after him and keeping him away from my mate. The vampire was fast though. He darted to the side when I lunged at him, my teeth snapping on air.

His shirt had ripped from our tussle and he finished the job, ripping it from hem to collar and discarding it on the ground. He was barely breathing hard and grinning like a maniac, red eyes bright with predatory delight.

"I had no desire to hurt your little human, werewolf." He planted his feet wide, arms out to the sides. "But you should have taken my deal. Now, there's no going back."

Thorne's hands morphed, growing nearly as large as my head, covered in black skin and tipped with long, black claws. The sight tripped me up, making me lose focus for a moment. I had no idea vampires could shift, if even just partially.

But I would deal with that information later. After I killed him.

The vampire drew his arms back and leaned his chest forward. I bared my teeth and growled with all my fury, fur spiking up over my back as all my muscles braced for this fight.

A fight that would surely end with one of us dead.

If that turned out to be me, I just hoped it would buy enough time for Emmaline to get to safety. The pack would look after her, I was sure of that.

A beat of time passed, the two of us tense and ready.

Wanting to catch the vampire off-guard, I lunged first.

But Thorne was ready for me and sliced those claws through the air, ready to shred me to ribbons.

CHAPTER 21

EMMALINE

I had never been so disoriented in my life. Dizziness, nausea, and fatigue ruled my senses. Even after something had grabbed my hair and yanked my head up, I didn't fully comprehend what was going on. I thought I saw Tryn as a wolf, *my* wolf, but how could that be possible? I had been in a city, not anywhere near Vargmore's picturesque forests.

Something inside me felt like it was frantically moving, a constant stampede or pacing sensation that wouldn't stop. It was making the nausea worse, and I found myself coughing into the dirt.

Wait...dirt.

My blurry vision could just make out my hands on a floor of grass, dirt, and leaf litter. I was outside, not in a dark alley in a city. With all my strength, I pushed myself up and tried to get my bearings. Relief and hope sprang in the form of tears filling my eyes.

The waning moon was bright, and the sky glittered

with stars. With the help of moonlight, I saw trees and mountains in the distance. I couldn't be sure but that looked like the same mountain range I saw from Stout & Spirit. Did the red-eyed man really bring me to Vargmore?

I started to turn around as my eyes adjusted to the darkness, finding more of the same. Trees, shrubs, hills, and mountains. Shit, what now?

It was only after I got a sense of where I was that I heard sounds coming from nearby. Growls, snarls, and yelps of pain, like animals fighting.

I held my breath, listening hard over the wild pounding of my heart. That urgent, frantic stamping feeling increased even more. I knew that it wasn't my heartbeat, but came from that sense of *another* inside of me. Whatever it was was freaking the fuck out.

A high-pitched cry of pain echoed through the trees and hills. That sound got me to my feet, this strange sense of urgency pushing me toward it, even though I was scared as hell and wanted nothing more than to run in the other direction. Who was I to get in the middle of an animal fight?

On shaky legs I followed the sounds up a gently rolling hill, telling myself all kinds of reasons why I'd be doing this. It was in my nature to help animals. If something was badly injured, I could help it.

But I also knew predators killed prey for food all the time. It was messy, bloody, and painful, but it was how the natural world worked. So who was I to save one animal and deprive another one of a meal?

Still I soldiered on, unable to fight this pull toward those sounds despite not understanding it in the least. The moment I crested the hill, my head remained in the dark. But my heart understood with painful, bleeding clarity.

Tryn was down there in his huge, beautiful wolf form. His teeth and muzzle were drenched in blood. His right foreleg was tucked close to his body and bleeding badly. More blood streaked through his fur, coating him so densely that I couldn't tell if it was his or his opponent's.

I almost didn't recognize the man, or creature, he fought. Tryn's opponent was shirtless, covered in lean, sinewy muscle and blood covering his torso. His hands were monstrous, at least three times the size of a normal man's hands, tipped with long, curving black claws like a bird's, and black skin up to his elbows.

It was only as Tryn and this monster circled each other that I realized it was the man from the dark alley. His red eyes were feral, upper canine teeth so long that they grazed his lower lip.

I didn't know what had happened or how I got here, but I knew one thing for certain—Tryn was protecting me.

And from the way he fought to maintain his balance on three good legs, his breaths coming in ragged pants through his clenched jaws, he wouldn't last much longer.

"Oh God…" I clamped a hand over my mouth to keep from calling out his name. The last thing he needed was to become distracted and allow that monster to land a killing blow on him.

After circling each other for a few tense seconds, they lunged at each other. I couldn't bring myself to look away as Tryn stopped short, using his hind legs to jump up toward the other creature's throat. It would have been a good move if his injuries weren't slowing him down. His opponent saw it coming and dodged out of the way. Then he casually, almost lazily, raked that huge, clawed hand down Tryn's side.

Tryn fell hard, his fresh wound coating more of his fur and the ground in blood. It was heartbreakingly clear he didn't have much fight left in him. I couldn't just watch, but what *could* I do?

Save him! The voice in my head called out. *Our mate needs us, help him!*

How? I screamed inside my mind. *I can't fight that thing any better than he can!*

Let me out! The stampeding sensation became so strong, it nearly brought me to my knees. I could physically feel pushing on my ribs, my back, my stomach, like a wild animal frantically trying to escape its cage.

My big, beautiful wolf got back on his feet, determined as ever. I couldn't let him die for me. He had to be in so much pain already. Knowing he was suffering for me, even after I reacted to him with fear and told him to leave, just about broke me.

"Tryn, stop," I whispered. "Just stop. Save yourself."

But he lunged again, catching the blackened skin of the creature's forearm and biting down savagely. As his opponent tried to shake him off, Tryn used the momentum to swing his back legs forward, raking his claws down the monster's torso.

"Ah, fucking dog!" The red-eyed creature lifted a foot and kicked Tryn squarely in the stomach, finally dislodging his teeth from his forearm.

Tryn had bitten down to the bone and ripped a good chunk of flesh away, but before my eyes, the bloody wound seemed to knit itself back together. I recalled Tryn healing quickly, but nowhere near *this* fast.

My wolf had rolled a few feet away after being kicked but was up again in the blink of an eye, although even more unsteady than before. Jesus, he just would not quit.

"You're boring me, werewolf," his opponent said. He was panting and still bleeding in some places but was nowhere near in the same condition as Tryn. "So I'm going to end you now and bring your mate back to my club as a snack for my men."

No! I screamed internally, frozen where I stood. *No, leave him alone!*

Tryn didn't seem fazed. He just lowered his head, golden eyes glaring with murderous intent, hackles raised in a spiky ridge along his back, and teeth bared. Badly injured as he was, he was still a terrifying sight to behold. Monstrous, even.

But he was *my* monster, and he was doing this for me. I felt none of the fear and confusion that had overwhelmed me when he shifted in my apartment. Without a single doubt, I knew that Tryn would never turn this aggression onto me, only those who would seek to harm me, like this red-eyed demon.

This time, the demon lunged first, aiming low. Tryn sprang forward, once again for the creature's throat.

"No!" I cried out this time, realizing his error too late.

He had exposed his belly to those claws. Instead of raking them down, the creature stabbed, embedding those curving talons deep into Tryn's flesh.

Time seemed to stop. The two of them were perfectly still for a beat, almost as if neither one knew what had happened.

Then the demon grinned, his eyes alight with victory, and he violently wrenched his claws from my werewolf's body.

Blood and flesh filled the air before raining to the ground.

CHAPTER 22

EMMALINE

I was running before becoming aware of traveling any distance. It was some miracle I was able to keep my feet under me. This other presence inside me was clawing, howling, stamping, running. It didn't entirely feel like I had control of my own body. But somehow, I made it to Tryn's side.

He lay motionless on the blood-soaked ground, and I slid a few inches when I dropped to my knees. My motions were on autopilot, ripping off my coat and shirt to press against the jagged, bleeding wounds on his abdomen. I wasn't treating him like an animal but someone I loved and desperately wanted to save.

"I'm here, I'm here." I leaned over and kissed the side of his face, petting his ears and stroking his fur with my free hand. "I'm so sorry, Tryn. I'm sorry. I shouldn't have told you to leave."

A pained groan rolled out of his throat and he wearily lifted his head, the wolf's golden eyes visibly widening in shock when they landed on me.

"I know," I told him as I stroked his muzzle. "It's okay. You're gonna be okay."

I was in shock, feeling a weird separation from my body. The wounds were deep and without immediate surgery, probably fatal. Plus, that demon was probably standing right behind me, getting a kick out of watching this heart-breaking moment.

My mate was dying, and what else could I do but stay with him and hold him?

Tryn let out a pained, wheezing huff of breath. Then, with what had to be a miraculous feat of strength, he started shifting into his human form.

"It's okay, you don't have to do that," I said.

But he'd already seen it through, and I was now staring at the ashen face of the man I'd fallen in love with.

"Emma...line," he whispered, pain lancing his words. "Run...you have to...run."

"I'm not leaving you."

I checked his abdomen to see if the shift had affected his wounds at all. They were still bleeding at the same rate, if not worse than before. I folded my jacket over to apply more pressure and added the weight of his good hand to mine. If we slowed the bleeding enough, maybe that would allow enough time for help to come.

"Derric...the pack..." A grimace twisted up Tryn's features. "The pack will...take care of you..."

"*You're* going to take care of me," I corrected. "Because you're going to heal. And I'm going to take care of you. We look after each other because we're mates, right?" I leaned down and pressed my forehead to his, not knowing how or why it felt so natural to say *mates*. "That's what we do, put each other first, don't we?"

An exhausted, pained smile pulled at Tryn's lips. "Yes…always."

"So you're going to keep pressure over these holes in your stomach until I can fix you, okay?" I stroked his cheek, staring intently at his unfocused eyes and paling skin. "And you're going to stay awake. Stay with me, Tryn."

He was looking worse by the minute and still continued doing his best to stay strong. Stubbornly, he opened his mouth to speak again. "Run," he croaked. "He'll…kill you."

"Well, I don't want a life without you." Tears fell freely, tracking through the blood covering his skin. "So I'm staying with you. My mate."

Everything clicked into place in that moment. All that I had been searching for, waiting for, was right here. The unconditional acceptance, love, and fulfillment that I'd been seeking was with him. A biker werewolf from a hidden world full of magic and monsters was the last thing I'd expected to make my life make sense, but that was exactly what Tryn did. He was my soft place to land, my home, and the source of all the love I'd been craving. I crashed into him, literally, right when I needed him. I was just too blind to see it right away.

I'd been too blind, too skeptical, too cautious the whole time we were together. I'd seen the truth too late, and now he was bleeding out on the forest floor.

"I'm so sorry," I sobbed, leaning over him.

"No…don't…" he groaned.

I thought he was telling me not to apologize until I heard boots crunching over dead leaves. My whole body froze as I felt the oppressive force of that monster looming over me.

"This is all very touching," the creature said. "But once

again, I'm bored and I'd like to spend my night doing other things. Sorry, little human. It's nothing personal—"

I whipped around to face him, and whatever he saw in my face abruptly made him stop talking. I wasn't sure how my face looked, but I felt different. Something inside me was changing, breaking free past a barrier I didn't know existed until now.

The voice that I'd heard inside my head for weeks now used my mouth to speak. "You've made an attempt on my mate's life. You will answer for this, vampire."

Vampire? Okay, I guess that made sense.

Said vampire's brows furrowed like he was confused. "I thought you were human."

"I am."

But I'm also a wolf.

The last of the barrier fell away, and the presence that had been awake and prowling inside me burst forth.

My wolf erupted from her hidden, dormant state like she'd been shot out of a cannon. The shift took over me so quickly, I was barely aware that it had happened. The wolf had full control, and I was happy to give it to her.

My beast was awake, free, and out for vengeance.

And she was fucking furious.

I came at the vampire so fast, he didn't have time to react. My head crashed into his sternum, sending him falling backwards. I didn't give him a chance to stand, rushing him in the blink of an eye before clamping my jaws down on his side. My teeth sank into lean muscle and flesh and I shook violently, intent on tearing off a piece of this vampire like he'd torn into my mate.

Hands closed around my throat and squeezed, cutting off my air, but I still didn't release him until my jaws went numb and I started to feel faint. The vampire must have thrown me, because I felt weightless for a moment before my whole body got slapped hard.

I coughed and wheezed, fighting for every precious breath as I rolled to all fours, then charged at the vampire again. He'd bought himself a few seconds, but he wasn't as fast as before. His injuries and fatigue from fighting Tryn must have been catching up to him, slowing him down.

My wolf, on the other hand, brimmed with fresh, predatory vigor. This was her first time feeling the ground on her paws and the breeze in her fur. She had the energy of a puppy and the seething rage of a bull. She'd chase this vampire all night long if she had to.

I went for his ankles this time, tripping him up and making him stumble. Once he hit the ground again, I dove for his throat. He anticipated the move and kicked me square in the chest. I didn't even feel it, I was so amped up on adrenaline and avenging my mate.

There was just no stopping my wolf, and the vampire was getting overwhelmed by my attacks. All the while, she roared in my head.

My mate's blood is on your hands, vampire! Die, die with your blood on my teeth! May your last thoughts be your regrets of ever laying a filthy hand on him.

"Fuck!"

The vampire brought his forearms and massive hands up to protect himself, swinging them every so often to shove me away, but I just kept coming back again and again. He was able to scratch me a few times enough to draw blood, but they were surface wounds and nowhere near enough to slow down my assault.

I was in a complete frenzy, nothing but a vengeful force

of nature with teeth and claws. I would not stop until this creature was dead and lifeless.

The vampire landed one good kick to my head that sent me sprawling. *Get up. Find him. Kill him,* my wolf insisted, but I was dizzy and disoriented. Precious seconds ticked by as I finally got to all fours and spotted the vampire running. He was bleeding heavily from his side, limping as ran, but was still inhumanely fast. I could catch up to him, if I just—

Stop, female. Do not chase him.

A voice that definitely wasn't my own or my wolf's reverberated in my head like a loudspeaker. It seemed to lock all my limbs in place, forcing me to obey the command. I growled in frustration, watching the vampire get smaller in the distance.

The voice came again, gentler this time. *This is Derric, Alpha of Howling Death. I'm giving you an Alpha command. Turn around and return to us. We will keep you safe.*

My body moved as if manipulated by a giant hand instead of my own will. Surrounding Tryn's body were four wolves, their ears pricked and eyes alert on me. Behind them, I recognized two of the men I'd met at Stout & Spirit sitting astride large motorcycles. One was heading toward Tryn with a large metal box, likely a first aid kit. The other stayed on his bike, eyes scanning the dark landscape as if on guard duty.

The biggest wolf, a massive beast covered in scars, stepped closer to me as he sniffed the air. *You saved our packmate, and we owe you a great debt. But I don't recognize you, female. Can you tell me who you are?*

I tried projecting my thoughts toward him. *It's me, Emmaline. Tryn's...mate.*

The giant wolf startled and let out a soft *whuff* that

sounded like surprise. He recovered quickly though, and his jaws parted in a canine smile. *So, you're one of us after all.*

I guess so. I could move freely now, my front paws tapping nervously on the ground. *How is Tryn? Will he make it?*

We need your medical skills and human hands to tell us that, Derric said gravely. *Do you have a set of clothes?*

Oh, um...

I looked around, seeing only shapeless scraps of fabric scattered across the ground. My clothes must have gotten torn up during that first shift.

It's alright, we should have something you can borrow. Do you need me to walk you through shifting back? We'll turn around to give you privacy.

Shifting back was easier than I expected. My wolf simply retreated and allowed my human side to take over once again. It still hadn't really sunk in that I was a shifter. I'd allow myself time to properly acknowledge it later. Right then, I had someone I desperately needed to save.

CHAPTER 23

TRYN

I never expected to wake up. The first coherent thought that arose when I did was that I hoped Emmaline got to safety. That Thorne, that filthy piece of shit vampire, never touched another hair on her head.

When her sweet blackberry scent entered my nose, stronger than it had ever been before, I thought I must still be dreaming. I fought to stay in that world, that imaginary place where a vampire had never gotten his hands on her and I had never scared her away with my shift.

I could be a human. Maybe that was my fate all along and I'd epically fucked it up. I'd give up being a wolf in a heartbeat if it meant I could keep my human mate forever.

"Tryn?"

Sweet moon, her voice sounded so real too. So strong and close by. I could practically feel her lips hovering by my ear.

"Are you waking up?"

The next thing I felt was warm lips on my forehead, and

the sensation pulled me all the way into the world of the living. I opened my eyes and saw her there.

"Emmaline," I croaked, reaching for her. She looked exhausted, her brow furrowed with worry, but fuck me, she was *here*. I didn't care if we were prisoners in a vampire den, as long as she was okay.

"Easy. Don't move." Her hands pressed to my shoulders and with surprising strength, laid me down flat. "You've been out for a few days, so take it really, really slowly."

"Ugh, fuck." As soon as my head hit the pillow, vertigo and nausea set in. "What happened?"

"You scared everyone to death, Bear."

My head snapped to the opposite side of the bed where Gran sat in a rocking chair. She put her tea and paperback aside before fixing me with a grin. "Welcome back."

"Uh, thanks." I looked at Emmaline and then back at Gran. "So, you two have met?"

"More than that." Emmaline chuckled. "Your Gran, Shiloh, and I spent hours elbows-deep inside you."

"That's, uh, frightening."

"In your abdomen," Gran clarified. "You lost a lot of blood and sustained serious damage to your internal organs. Shiloh and I kept you together with herbs and magic. Your little mate over there is quite the surgeon. She did all the dirty work."

Emmaline dipped her head with a smile. "I couldn't have done it without the two best witches at my side. So yeah, you could say your Gran and I are very well-acquainted now."

"I wasn't *just* talking about operating on him, dear." Gran's eyes twinkled. "The whole pack can't stop howling about how you sent that vampire running like a cockroach."

"The vampire?" I stared at Emmaline. "Running, how? You didn't...fight him, did you?"

"Well..." She chewed her lip, eyes darting toward Gran, who stood from her rocking chair with a groan.

"I'll leave you kids to that discussion." Gran gathered up her things, then bent over me to kiss my forehead. "I knew you wouldn't leave her, Bear," she whispered in my ear. "Your fate thread was the strongest, brightest I've ever seen. The moon chose well for you." She patted my cheek, then with a quick hug to Emmaline, left my room.

Once we were alone, Emmaline looked nervous. Not in a bad way, but in a giddy, brimming-with-excitement kind of way.

"So what happened with the vampire?" I asked, watching her stand from the side of the bed.

She chewed her lip, fiddling with the buttons on her shirt. "I should probably just show you."

"Okay..." I only grew more confused as she walked to the foot of my bed.

My mate undressed in a fast, efficient way and I forgot all about vampires and nearly dying. She bared herself to me, all slender curves and swooping lines that formed the shape of the woman that was meant for me. The sight of her naked body took my breath away and I ached to touch her.

"Emmaline," I rasped.

She held up a hand. "Give me a second. I'm still getting used to this." Her eyes closed and she started a series of deep breaths.

Come here, were the next words on my tongue, but they never made it out with what happened next.

Her form changed. She *shifted* right before my very eyes.

In place of the woman I had gotten to know and love, stood the most beautiful wolf I'd ever seen. Her fur was predominantly a cream color on her chest, legs, and belly, with a pattern of browns and grays coating her ears, back and tail.

Emmaline's wolf placed her forepaws on my bedside, round amber eyes meeting mine with a shy, hopeful stare. Her tail swished slowly back and forth with cautious excitement.

"Holy...shit." I whispered in awe. "Fuck me, Emmaline. You're so...fucking moon, you're fucking stunning."

She let out a soft, happy bark and jumped on my bed, giving my face a lick before settling next to me.

"Oh, look at you." I massaged the fur at her scruff, then stroked down her back. I had to blink tears away and couldn't stop marveling, couldn't believe my luck that this was real. "You're such a beautiful, vicious thing, aren't you?"

Emmaline's wolf snorted and gave a playful nip of my fingers. She was on the smaller side, as most females were, but my wolf sensed a ferocity in her that he immediately adored. She was scrappy, a cunning predator that had already won her first fight. This pretty little thing had been lying dormant, caged up for too long, and there was a snappy reactivity in her.

"You're safe with the pack," I assured her. "Anyone who tries to fuck with you is a damn fool, aren't they?"

She nudged her nose into my palm and licked me there with a soft whine. Her body language was clear. *It's not me I'm worried about.*

"No one's coming after me either." I scratched the side of her neck. "The vampires want access to the angel's city for some reason. I think Thorne found you and it was the most convenient way to try to strike a deal." I frowned at the thought. Our business with the vampires and angels wasn't over.

Emmaline shifted back to her human form. Now, as a naked woman lying next to me, she brought her hands under her head to use as a pillow. "I went looking for Stout & Spirit because I needed to talk to someone about what you showed me." She let out a little scoff and rolled her eyes. "I thought I could follow the same path you took on the bike, but that was a really stupid idea, in hindsight. I guess I took a few wrong turns and yeah, ended up in a city of angels."

"So Thorne *did* find you there?"

She nodded. "I told Derric everything. I stumbled across Thorne in a really seedy area, in a dark alley." She curled up, bringing her legs toward her chest. "Derric explained that vampires are violating some kind of agreement by sneaking into the city."

"That's right. Now that we have a reliable witness in you, and the fact that he tried to cut a deal with me, we know for sure something's going on. And we can support the angels better."

Emmaline scooted closer and higher up the bed until her head rested on my shoulder. "I would've killed him. I *wanted* to kill him. I woke up and saw...what he did to you." She let out an adorable little growl that I knew was her wolf speaking her agreement. "Derric explained that the fight took place within the bounds of the vampire territory. He stopped me because the vampires would retaliate if we killed their leader on their home turf."

I chuckled and pressed a kiss to her hair. "Sorry you

didn't get your kill. We'll go for a hunt as soon as I'm cleared by my veterinarian."

Emmaline laughed. "I'm still blown away by how fast you—I mean, we—heal. At this rate, you'll be good as new by the end of the week."

"Excellent news." I ran my thumb along her jaw, tilting her face up toward mine. "What I don't understand though, is how you were able to shift. I thought you needed a bite from me."

"Yeah, that took a lot of people by surprise." She laughed lightly. "I talked with your Gran, who talked to a bunch of other witches, and some of the elder wolves. Their theory is my wolf forced her way out when she realized your life was in jeopardy. She—I, we faced a very real danger of losing you, and that triggered a reaction that gave her dominance over my human side." Emmaline cocked her head. "Apparently it's happened before, but it's incredibly rare because it has to be triggered by very specific, dire circumstances. Your Gran said there was a document over a thousand years old that seemed to allude to a similar thing, but it's in a language hardly anyone speaks anymore, so no one is certain."

"So what you're telling me is," I gazed at her face, stroking her cheek. "Not only are you brilliant, brave, and beautiful, you're also a miracle worker."

"Nothing of the sort," she scoffed. "I just couldn't afford to lose you."

"And I couldn't let him take you," I said. "Thank the moon you could hold your own against him. He was not fucking ready."

She chuckled. "No, he wasn't."

We were quiet for a few moments. Emmaline slipped

under my blanket and sheets to nestle against me, her bare skin radiating the heat of a fully-realized shifter.

My mate, a werewolf after all.

As joyous as the thought was, it also gave me pause. Emmaline seemed happy and content now, but I couldn't forget the last time we had seen each other. The fear and bewilderment in her eyes when I shifted in her apartment.

"How are you feeling about all this?" I asked with a tight throat. "Being a shifter yourself, knowing that vampires and angels also exist. You were pretty over-whelmed the last time we talked about it."

"I was," she said softly. "But the shock wore off pretty quickly, and once it did, I wanted to know more. I wanted to understand. That was why I went looking for Stout & Spirit, I wanted to talk to others about it. Mainly Riley, and maybe Shiloh too. It wasn't that I *didn't* want to see you, I just wanted more perspectives."

"Sure, that makes sense," I hedged.

Emmaline rubbed absently over her sternum. Our fate thread glittered like a silver-lined rope as her hand passed through it.

"I didn't realize it at the time, but I had been hearing and listening to my wolf ever since I met you," she went on. "I felt this...restless presence inside me that always pulled me to you. I heard a voice that felt like my own thoughts but also separate from 'me', you know?"

"Welcome to life as a shifter," I chuckled. "It's like sharing a body and brain with an imaginary friend. Only that friend is also you, kind of. There is some overlap between you and your wolf, but it's totally possible to have completely separate desires from each other."

"That's exactly what it was. She must have sensed your

wolf and constantly wanted to get close to you. To...bite you." Emmaline blushed. "But my human side was trying to be cautious and not rush into things."

"There's nothing wrong with that, either," I said. "We can still take things slow. Date and see each other the human way. I'm happy with whatever you want to do."

The words seemed to punch their way out of me, leaving a painful ache where they left. After everything we'd been through, the slow, human way felt like torture.

Emmaline was meant for me. She was one of my kind and, with the exception of my gift, knew almost every truth about me. *Why bother with slow when the moon Herself had tied our fates together?* my wolf wondered with a disgruntled huff.

But if it was what my mate wanted, I would do it.

"No." Emmaline sat up abruptly, pinning me with an intense expression.

I returned her stare, unsure what to feel about that simple word that held an incredible weight. "No?"

She shook her head, a grin pulling at her lips. "It all clicked into place for me right before I shifted for the first time. I'm not human. All my life I've never fit in with humans. Even in vet school, when I was among other animal science nerds, I found it hard to connect with my classmates. I always thought it had to do with the culture I grew up in, personalities I didn't click with, my parents trying to force me down a certain path, and maybe all that's true to an extent, but the simple fact is, I'm not one of them. I'm one of you."

Emmaline leaned closer to me, her hand on my cheek. "I was drawn to you when I first met your wolf. Then when I met you as a man, and you talked about Vargmore, I felt so...*homesick*, for a place I'd never been before. The way you talked so fondly about your home, I would've given anything to have that for myself."

"It's yours," I told her, hope brimming in my voice. "This can be your home. With me."

She nodded, leaning closer until her forehead touched mine. "And my wolf's instincts were right all along. You are my home, Tryn. It's you I belong with. It doesn't matter if we're running as wolves or riding on your motorcycle. You found me and...everything finally made sense."

"My beautiful, brilliant mate. It's the same for me." I traced her cheekbone with my thumb and inhaled her intoxicating scent, now no longer hidden under layers of human. "You are the greatest gift the moon has ever given me. Everyone dreams of meeting their mate, but I never could have imagined someone as incredible as you." Our lips met in a brief kiss before I added in a low growl, "And with such a savage little wolf under her skin."

Emmaline grinned, her voice also taking on a growl. "I will rip the throat and fangs out of any vampire that gets near my mate again."

"Okay, seriously. Am I cleared for sexual activity? Because your murder talk is absolutely doing it for me."

She laughed lightly, returning to lie next to me. "Not yet, I'm afraid. We redressed your wounds this morning. Those claws of his must have been filthy because Shiloh and your Gran have been working overtime to keep infection away."

"Damn." I leaned back on my pillows with a sigh. "How long has it been since the fight?"

"Three days." Emmaline brought her head to my

shoulder and her arm across my chest. "We'll see how it looks tomorrow."

"Hmm, fine." I rested my cheek on top of her head, running a touch from her arm to her shoulder. Sex would've been great and all, but I wasn't truly bothered. My mate was here, and that was all that mattered. She had chosen me after all.

But inside my skin, my wolf paced impatiently.

I know, I told him. *Once my insides are no longer in danger of falling out, we'll give her our bite. Just a little longer.*

He answered me with a disgruntled huff and a short howl of yearning.

CHAPTER 24

EMMALINE

I hunkered low to the ground, my fur blending in with the forest. Neither my breaths nor my paws made a sound as I stalked my prey, a fat quail scratching in the leaf litter for grubs.

Get as close as you can without it noticing, Tryn instructed. *When you can't get any closer, then you strike.*

I took another step and...*crack.*

My paw landed on a dried leaf, which crackled like a potato chip and sent my prey scurrying, then flying into the tree canopy.

Damn it! I howled out my frustration while Tryn came up to my side and gave me an affectionate bump of his forehead against my cheek

It just takes practice. You never had the chance to hunt as a pup. He licked my face, his wolf making soft huffing noises as if trying to reassure me. *You got a lot closer that time.*

You said not to take my eyes off it, but if I don't, how will I learn not to step on dead leaves? I grumbled.

Over time, your wolf will learn where and how to place her

paws. She's learning to be a hunter too, developing her instincts. Let go and trust her.

He was right, of course. It didn't mean I wasn't frustrated. I sat on my haunches and started to groom myself.

Tryn's human voice chuckled in my head as he nuzzled me and licked my ear. *Done for the day?*

Yes, please. Hunting was hard work, and we'd been practicing every day since his wounds had fully healed three days ago. I loved my animal side the more I got to know her, but I still loved human comforts just as much. Such as popping an easy meal into the microwave or sleeping in a bed.

Good. Tryn's voice brimmed with excitement. *Catch me.*

Without another word, he darted off through the forest. For such a large wolf, he sure could move fast.

Tryn, come on! I called.

This was another lesson, of course. He wanted me to follow him by scent. At least I was miles better at tracking than hunting.

I allowed my wolf to lead the way, which she was happy to do. Once she was certain Tryn would survive his injuries, so much of her pent-up aggression had melted away. When she was relaxed and not sensing any threats, she was actually a happy-go-lucky girl.

One side effect of her being latent for so long was that she found it difficult to focus on one scent. She wanted to pursue *every* scent trail she came across, from the rotting log a few feet away, to the family of deer that had crossed through here a few hours ago, to the mysterious feral wolf packs that stayed hidden away in the mountains. Every trail was a new adventure and she wanted to go on *all* of them.

It was up to my human side to keep her on course.

Tryn's trail, I reminded her. *Follow your mate. We'll go on an adventure next time.*

She was happy to oblige, and we soon found Tryn in a clearing with a grassy field dotted with wild flowers and a small lake nearby. Like he had planned this ahead of time, he had shifted to his human form and was rolling out a picnic blanket on the bank of the lake.

"Hi, beautiful," he said when I approached, scratching behind my ears.

My wolf absolutely loved his praise. She preened and stretched, bumping her head against his palm.

"Do you recognize this place?" He settled onto the blanket, stretching out long in all his naked, masculine glory.

I shifted as well to lie next to him. "No. I've never been here, silly."

"Not here, exactly." He pointed to a rocky ridge in the distance. "But remember when I took you there?"

It took a moment for the information to settle in. "Our first date?"

He grinned.

"Are you serious?" I turned on my side to face him. "That very first time you took me out, you were showing me Vargmore?"

"I was," he said softly. "I knew from the very beginning you were going to be important to me."

"The wolves we saw. Was that Howling Death? Did you ask them to show up so I could see them?"

He grinned. "It didn't take a lot of convincing, but I owe the guys a few more rounds at Stout & Spirit for that."

"That's...oh my God." I rolled to my back, laughing. "I can't believe you arranged something like that on our first date."

"What can I say? You liked wolves, and I wanted you to like me." He propped himself on one elbow, caressing my side and waist with one hand.

"I more than like you, Tryn."

I rolled into his touch, sliding right up against his chest. My heart pounded against the heated kiss of his skin on mine. I was gearing myself up, getting ready to say exactly what I meant by more-than-like. My lips parted as I pulled in a breath and—

"There's something else you should know about me."

I closed my mouth abruptly, looking at Tryn's face with concern. "What's up?"

His chest expanded with the depth of his inhale. "Gran has a pretty unique ability as a witch. And even though she's the only non-werewolf in my family, it seems Gran's ability got passed down to me."

"Okay." I slid an arm over his waist and stroked his back. "What is it?"

Tryn cleared his throat. He seemed almost more nervous now than when he first shifted in front of me. "I can see things other people can't."

"Okay," I repeated. "Like what?"

"Most of what I see is threads. Everyone has several threads connected to them, and those threads have different qualities, depending on the person. For example, if someone is a habitual liar, their truth thread will be weak and all kinked up."

Wow. He just continued to fascinate me at every turn. "I see. So it's kind of like you can see certain aspects of people right away. For everyone else, it takes time to find out that information."

"Yeah, you could say that. I see other things that don't

always make sense either, but they always come to fruition." He told me about Laylah, the sister of the angel's leader, Camael, and how he saw puncture marks and blood on her neck.

"Holy shit," I breathed. "In one way, that's an incredible gift, but it must feel like such a burden to hold so much knowledge about people."

"It feels like a curse sometimes," he admitted. "I've never been able to block it out. It does help me to get a good read on people, and I've been able to help the pack at times. But yeah, sometimes it's all just too much."

"I'm sorry." I stretched up to kiss his neck just under his bearded jaw. "You can unload on me, if that would help."

"There's more," he said with an apologetic smile. "Can't you tell I'm stalling on the way to this big reveal I'm trying to make?"

"Oh, wow. Okay, I'm listening."

Tryn paused for a long time, rough fingers circling on my shoulder blade. "I can also see fate threads. The threads that connect two people who are meant to be together, as destined by fate." His fingers stopped moving. "I could never see my own threads, fate or otherwise, until a few days before you hit me with your car."

"I never did apologize to you for that, did I?" I laughed softly, grabbing his beard to kiss him. "I'm sorry, handsome. I'm so glad we met, but I wish it didn't have to be over injuring you with a two-ton hunk of metal." He didn't respond, and the true weight of what he was explaining about fate threads hit me right then. "Wait, so you're saying..."

"I followed my fate thread to the human world." Tryn brought his index finger to my chest, drawing down until he stopped right over my heart. "That was why I ran across that road that night. I followed the thread to find my fated mate."

His thumb and forefinger pinched close together but not touching. Then he drew his hand toward himself slowly, fingers close together as if he were gently running them along a length of string. His hand stopped when he reached his own heart. "I can see it now, in this space between us."

My heart thundered as the weight of what he was saying sank in. "Wait, *fated* mate? Is there a difference between being fated and just mates?"

"Well, mates can be any serious romantic pair. But being fated means we are meant for each other, predestined by forces outside our control."

I swallowed. "And that's...me?"

His hand fell to my waist again, giving me an affectionate squeeze. "Of course it's you. Who else would it be?"

"But you've known the whole time? Since the *very* beginning?"

"Since I woke up in that cage at your vet clinic and saw the thread that connected my heart to yours." He stilled, watching me carefully. "Are you upset?"

"Upset? God, no. I just...wow." I brought a palm to my forehead, thinking back to every interaction we'd ever had.

He sat next to me in the bar on purpose. Talked to me like he genuinely wanted to know me. Scared off Dr. Stone like the hero I didn't know I needed. He gave me his number to put the ball in my court and not pressure me. Showed me an incredible view and kissed me on an amazing first date without pushing for more.

"Good wow or bad wow?" Tryn looked anxious, trying to read my expression.

"Good. So, so good. I was just thinking back to everything and how you were so wonderful the whole time. You knew we were supposed to end up together but you never acted like it was given. You let me set the pace and never acted entitled to my time, my body, anything. Our relationship happened so...organically."

"I knew I had to be careful with you," he said softly, running his hand from my ribs to my hip. "Not only were we perfect strangers, we were from completely different worlds. I never wanted to drag you into something that you didn't fully understand or consent to." His hand came to my face, thumb stroking the corner of my jaw. "And of course I wanted to get to know you. Fated mates means forever. What good would rushing and forcing things do? We have forever to fall in love."

"Well, I didn't need forever." I caressed the edge of his beard, mirroring the way he touched me. "And while I can't see the thread between us, I think I knew on some level we were meant to be too. You just..." I swallowed past the knot of emotion in my throat. "You showed me who I really am."

Tryn's nose touched mine, his thick arms encircling me. "Are you saying you love me, Emmaline?"

"Yes." I sniffed and laughed through the happy tears squeezing onto my eyelashes. "Way to be romantic."

"I love you too, my ferocious, beautiful mate." He wiped my tears and kissed my brow. "I'm so glad you rammed into me and broke my leg."

"Hey now, it was a hairline fracture, which I still find unbelievable. You werewolves have some serious bone density."

"*We* werewolves," he corrected with a smirk.

"Yes, *we.*"

He held my chin and kissed me deeply, full of sensuality and want. When he pulled back, all smiles were gone and his gaze was intense, ablaze with hunger. "I love you, Emmaline. You've given my life meaning in ways you can't even imagine."

"I love you, Tryn. My mate." I tugged at his lower lip with my teeth on our next kiss, resulting in a deep, sexy groan from him.

"One last thing you need to know." His voice became rough, guttural as he rolled me to my back and fit himself on top of me.

"The bites." I stared at the thick, round muscle of his shoulder, already itching to sink my teeth into his flesh.

"Yes." His lips grazed my neck like he was thinking the same thing. "When mates bite each other, it solidifies the bond. Our fates will be sealed and our scents will change slightly to the perspective of other wolves. That scent change, and the scars from our bites, are like wedding bands for humans. They tell everyone we're taken and off-limits."

I wrapped my legs around his hips, using my thighs to squeeze and draw him in closer. "So what are we waiting for?"

He grinned against my neck before lifting to meet my eyes. "The bites make this permanent, Emmaline. For the rest of our lives, and we'll live for a *very* long time. Are you absolutely sure?"

"Yes." I had never been more sure of anything in my life, even becoming a vet. "This is me talking, not my wolf, Tryn.

I waited my whole life for you, and there's no doubt in my mind that I want my fate intertwined with yours forever."

He stared at me for a moment before resting his forehead on mine with a sigh. "Fuck. What did I do to deserve you?"

"Bite me and maybe it'll come to you." I nuzzled the side of his face until I found his earlobe and nipped it, pulling another delicious groan from him.

Tryn eased away from my teeth, mischief lighting up his eyes. "Here's the thing, beautiful."

"Ugh, what *now?*" I moaned with mock frustration.

His fist closed in my hair, prompting me to arch and bare my throat. "Every mated wolf I've talked to says the bites feel best when on the brink of orgasm."

CHAPTER 25

EMMALINE

The way he looked at me, caged under his thick, muscle bound body, was predatory in the absolute best way. He would only ever look at *me* like this, like the most savory, delectable meal he'd ever tasted. I was at the mercy of this big, powerful wolf and wouldn't want to be anywhere else.

Tryn's mouth fell to mine in a rough, possessive kiss that lit a fire throughout my nervous system. His bare skin slid against mine, eliciting a need for his touch everywhere. My arms slid around his back as the kiss deepened. With his rich scent in my nose, the pressure and slide of his lips and tongue, and how he trapped me beneath him, I was already getting drunk on pleasure from this wolf.

"Question," I gasped when his mouth slid away, dragging a trail of heat along my jaw to my neck.

"Mm." It was barely a sound over the kisses he placed along my pulse.

"How many orgasms before you bite me?"

He chuckled darkly, taking his time to suck lightly at the crook of my neck. "As many as I want."

"Rough estimate?"

"I'm thinking double digits."

"*Double digits?!* Tell me you're not serious."

"Haven't decided yet." He found my mouth and kissed me again, his grin only widening. "You act like my wanting to please you is a bad thing."

"You can please me all you want after you bite me." My nails dug into his back. "That's what I want most of all, Tryn. Your claim on me. I don't want to spend another moment not being officially yours."

"You make very strong arguments, Dr. E. I'll consider it." He nipped my lip before heading lower, trailing under my chin and nibbling at the column of my throat. "But I want to savor you," he added in a throaty whisper before kissing the space between my collarbones. "I want to taste and please and inhale every inch of my mate before I claim her. I'm going to become intimately acquainted with every square inch of her body. Only then can I decide where to place my bite."

"Fuck, you're going to kill me, aren't you?" Despite how long he intended to drag this out, my toes curled in antici-pation and I arched under the blissful treatment of his hands and mouth. If I didn't focus on the bite, having him worship and please me from head to toe sounded abso-lutely incredible.

"If I do, I'll make sure you enjoy every second of it," he promised. His lips dragged down my sternum before moving over to one breast.

I shivered at the rough contact of his beard, the soft breeze of warm air from his mouth, and the slightest searing heat from the tip of his tongue. He circled my flesh, ignoring my nipple until the peak was uncomfortably tight and tense. It ached so badly for contact, it was nearly painful. When he finally laved his tongue over it, I moaned with relief. Then pinpricks of pain returned as he dragged his teeth over it, and my moan turned into a sharp cry.

Tryn alternated sensations. Soft and soothing, then rough and sharp. It was maddening, delicious torture. When he finally dragged his mouth to my other breast to give it the same treatment, his hand continued what his mouth had begun.

Massaging, kneading, and caressing gave way to pinching and pulling. Hands and mouth left my skin reddened from all the attention. My mate was mauling me, and I loved it.

All of it heightened the pulsing between my legs to a needy, desperate level. My clit ached almost to the point of pain. He hadn't even touched me there yet and would barely need to to get me off.

"Tryn," I whined, squirming on the picnic blanket. "Enough. I need…"

"What do you need, my sweet fate?" He swept both breasts into his large hands and dragged his thumbs over my nipples.

"I need to come!"

"Oh, already?" He leaned down with a cocky grin, the ends of his hair tickling over my skin and making my desperation even worse.

"Yes! Please touch me."

"Hmm." He sat back on his heels, looking pensive while I felt on the verge of crying. "How about you touch yourself for me?"

"Touch...myself?" A fresh wave of heat licked over my body, brought on by desire and shyness in equal measure.

"Yeah, I'll give you this one." Tryn's gaze raked over my body, lips parted like he couldn't decide where to start devouring me. "Let me see how my girl makes herself come."

He didn't have to ask me twice. I felt shy under the intensity of his gaze, but the need for a release was stronger. My fingers pressed over my clit hood, and I let my eyes feast on the naked man kneeling in front of me just as he was to me.

Tryn was so incredibly built. Wide shoulders wrought with muscle that led down to powerful arms and huge hands that protected and touched me so well. His thick, barrel chest rose and fell with his breaths, his abs also flexing with the movement. His thighs were thick as well, and they *did* save my life, as the saying goes.

I held off looking at the most delectable part of him until I'd taken my fill of everything else. My self-control was surprising to me, but once I looked at his cock, my fingers pressing and circling my clit, I knew my release was imminent.

He was half-hard, thicker than my wrist, and long enough for me to wonder if my cervix was going to have some objections. But did I really care? Hell no. If we were fated mates, surely we were biologically compatible too.

"Spread your legs wider," Tryn growled. His cock flexed, doing a little jump as he spoke. "Let me see that sweet cunt as you make yourself come."

I planted my feet a few more inches apart, but apparently that wasn't enough.

"More. Let me see all of you."

Before I could do anything else, Tryn scooted forward on his knees and palmed my inner thighs with those huge hands of his. He pressed both legs out to the side until my knees hit the blanket. I could not be more spread open and exposed than this.

"Oh fuck yes, keep going," he murmured, eyes glued to where my hand was. "You're so fucking wet. That pretty pussy is so glossy for me." His hands remained clamped on my thighs, his cock growing stiffer by the second. If he came forward another few inches, he'd have that blunt head inside me.

A strike of pleasure hit me so hard, I gasped for breath. My legs pressed against Tryn's hands, wanting to snap closed, but he wouldn't let me. The building pressure was getting to be too much, a few more swipes and I'd be done for. But my werewolf knew how to prolong and build up my pleasure even when he wasn't the one touching me.

"Stop for a second. Spread your lips and let me see you. Fuck, that's beautiful." He swallowed and licked his lips, tightening his grip on my thighs. Any more and he'd leave bruises on my flesh, but like I cared.

"Finger yourself for me, as deep as you can go. Oh yeah, like that. Sweet moon, fuck." He released one of my legs to fist his cock, spreading the bead of precum that formed at the tip.

That sight alone ratcheted up my pleasure even more. I was teetering on the precipice, *just* on the verge of falling.

"Tryn, don't stop." My hips bucked against my own touch. I lifted my head to see him better, to watch him stroke himself as he was to me.

He grinned salaciously, canting his hips in small thrusts

as he fucked into his palm. "You like watching me too, beautiful?"

"Fuck yes," I panted, my breath tight. "You're going to make me come."

"You're the most gorgeous creature I've ever seen," he moaned, quickening the pace of his hand. "You're going to make me explode, Emmaline."

"I want to see, Tryn. I want to feel it, your cum on my skin." Right then, I needed to see and feel his release more than I needed food or air.

"By the fucking moon, Emmaline." His head tipped back with a moan, exposing the long, sexy column of his throat.

"No, watch me." I was surprised by how commanding my own voice sounded. "You wanted to see me come, so keep those eyes on me."

He faced forward again, grinning in apparent pleasure at my bossiness. "Yes, my sweet fate. Tell me everything you want because I am utterly fucking yours. You *own* me, body and soul."

"Come on me," I begged. "Cover me in your release, your scent. I want you coating my skin."

"Holy fucking shit," he growled, his hand pumping his cock so fast, it became a blur.

I wanted to arch my head back but forced my gaze to stay on him. The hottest fantasy in my head could never come close to the real thing. The sounds he made, all harsh breaths and deep, masculine moans. The flush of his tan skin, the deep crease in his brow, the muscles jumping in his chest, arm, and stomach. He was real. He was mine. And it was him that sent my pleasure shooting off like a rocket.

My pinned thigh shook under his grip, and the tremors

licked up my spine and down to my toes. Heat poured over me as deep pulses rang out through my body. I could barely feel the ground under my back with the floating sensation that overtook me.

Tryn's rough moans and curses brought me back down to earth, and the sight of him alone was almost enough to set me off again.

He jerked his cock furiously, hips stuttering into an unsteady rhythm. When the first rope of cum lashed my belly, he let out a strangled cry of relief. He let go of my leg to plant his hand next to me while he wrung out his release all over my skin, painting my stomach, my breasts, all the way up to my collarbones. His spend was hot to the touch, like fingers stroking over my cooled skin.

Tryn looked absolutely wrecked when he finished, arm muscles shaking to hold himself up. My werewolf leaned his forehead on my knee while his stomach contracted with every ragged breath.

"Fuck, the way you look right now." He shook his head as if in disbelief, a lazy smile coming to his lips. "Flushed with your orgasm, covered in my cum. You're a vision, Emmaline."

I smiled, reaching up to push his hair back. "You know what would make me look even better?"

Tryn's face dropped the blissed out smile immediately, hardening into something sharp and predatory. "Beg for bites again and I'll drop you in the pond."

"You wouldn't," I gasped.

"Try me," he challenged.

"It's just that we've both already come and—fuck! Tryn!"

He shut my legs together, hauled me up from the blanket, and literally threw me over his shoulder. Who would have thought my werewolf was also a caveman?

"Tryn, put me down!" I screamed through laughter, pounding with little force at his back.

He slapped my ass in return. "I warned you, sweetheart."

Ignoring my protests, he walked us both into the freezing cold pond until we were chest-deep. He let me slide down his torso so I could wrap my arms and legs around him.

"Might as well wash up for the next round," he mused, taking my chin in his hand before kissing me.

"Next round?" His mouth was deliciously hot compared to the chilly water.

"I told you," he growled. "You're getting an undetermined amount of orgasms before you get the one that includes my bite." He palmed my ass, lifting me to run my pussy along the length of his cock, which was already hardening again.

"Jesus Christ," I moaned, letting my head roll back.

Tryn laughed with a nip to my throat. "I'm just getting started with you, my sweet fate."

CHAPTER 26

TRYN

I carried Emmaline out of the water before the chilly temperature became too much. She shivered slightly, and her skin was covered in goosebumps. Not to worry, she'd be properly warmed up in minutes.

"I don't suppose you brought towels?" She immediately curled up into a ball when I set her on the picnic blanket.

"Nope. We're air-drying." I held her against my chest, arms and legs wrapped around her. "Let your wolf rise up a bit. She can withstand the cold better than your human side can."

Within seconds, she stopped shivering and her breaths no longer shook. "Wow, that feels so much better." She rubbed her chest. "I feel her so vividly now. Do you always keep your wolf this close to the surface?"

"Generally, yes. We'll rely on our wolf's senses even when we're in human form. She's not going to take over unless it's right around the full moon. You'll get used to her being there."

Emmaline leaned back, resting her head on my

shoulder and her slight weight against my chest. "It's so incredible what we are, isn't it?"

"Yeah, I like it alright." My hands slid across her waist and her belly. "Especially now that I've found you."

She looked up with a smile. "Technically I found you first, didn't I?"

"Your front bumper sure as shit found my leg, I'll give you that."

She laughed and our mouths came together in a kiss. My touch ventured over her slick, naked skin, savoring her just as I said I would. It still blew my mind that she chose *me*. This brilliant, beautiful woman, who made me explode from her touching herself and was in my arms right now, was mine to cherish and protect forever.

One palm stroked up to her breast, catching her nipple between my thumb and forefinger while the other hand slid down low over her belly and mound. The sensitive peak was taut and stiff from the cold water, but her cunt burned hot and slick as ever.

"Tryn." Emmaline's gasp of my name was so pretty, so fucking hot. She squirmed in my hold, thrusting her ass against my cock.

"Fuck me, you're soaked and it's all you, beautiful." I stroked and teased her pussy, knowing how sensitive she must have been from the first orgasm. "Nothing to do with the water, that's your sweet cunt dripping for me." I rasped against her ear, loving the small jerks of her body and her gasps of breath. "You feel how hard you're making me? You feel how bad I want to sink inside of you?"

My mouth fell to the crook of her neck and I sucked a hard kiss there, dragging my teeth along her skin.

Bite her, my wolf howled. *Our sweet mate has waited so long. It's all she wants.*

Not yet, I told him.

While kissing and nipping her neck, I rubbed Emmaline's clit just as she had done to herself until another orgasm shuddered through her. Instead of watching a sexy spread-open view, I felt the effects of her pleasure in my arms. My cock turned to steel as her body jerked, shuddered, and collapsed limply. Her skin was hot and completely dry now, except for a few beads of sweat at her temple.

"Fucking moon, your scent," I moaned, removing her from my embrace before turning her around to face me.

"Tryn, what—Oh God!"

She got the picture the moment I grabbed her hips and dove to seal my mouth over her pussy. Her scent, now clear and unhindered by her human chemistry, had been tantalizing me since we started kissing out here. I had thought of licking her to her first orgasm, but the sight of her spread open with her hand between her legs was too good. I wanted it burned into my memory.

The water had washed off some of her scent to the point where I could almost ignore it, but after her second orgasm, all bets were off. She blossomed like a flower in spring, a flower I wanted to suck and lick and drink from until my lips fell off.

I kept my tongue away from her clit for a while, knowing she'd be overstimulated to the point of pain if I touched that little nub before it had enough rest. That was no issue, as I had plenty to love on between her legs. Her lips were plump and so slick with her cum. I tugged on them, kissing as I would her mouth. I pressed my tongue inside her, licking and tasting the place where my cock would be soon.

A few times, I was even nice enough to leave her pussy alone entirely for a bit of reprieve. I sucked the sensitive flesh just to the sides of her cunt instead or kissed her inner thighs with plenty of teeth until she trembled again.

Emmaline kept trying to close her legs around my head, but I held her spread open as I feasted on her. I wanted to ravage her until she couldn't come anymore and then bathe in her scent. Aside from the bite marks, wearing the scent of your mate was the best way to tell others that you were off-limits.

Time didn't exist as I devoured the sweetest meal I'd ever tasted. It was just me and this perfect little pussy over-powering all of my senses.

Eventually I felt nails raking over my scalp, fingers curling in my hair and tugging, urging me higher. With a loud sucking sound, I broke away and leaned against Emmaline's leg.

"Hi, beautiful." I hugged around her leg with one arm and placed a long, sensual kiss on her thigh. "I'm a little busy here. Did you need something?"

Her head fell back as her whole body shook with laughter, her breasts jiggling hypnotically.

"You ass, you know I'm dying to come."

"Oh, really? I'm happy to oblige." I grinned at her flushed, frustrated expression. "That'll be number three now, won't it?"

"Tryn, come *on*. Please."

There was something so sweet about her begging. I had to resist the urge to grab my cock again before sliding low to where I'd just been.

"Come on my tongue, beautiful. Just one more, then I'll give you what you really need."

"Promise?"

"I swear, my love. You'll have my bite after this one."

After how badly I'd hurt her before, I'd never lie to her again. Not a single fucking word of untruth would pass from my lips to my mate.

I slid my mouth over her cunt again, moaning against her skin as I savored her sweet flavor. This time, I focused my tongue on her clit. She quaked so beautifully under my ministrations, and I allowed her thighs to clamp around my head. When she finally exploded, gushing into my mouth, I didn't let up feasting on her until she brought a hand down and yanked me away with a fist in my hair.

Licking my lips, I grinned as I rose up to kneeling. "Still not done with you."

She was limp and panting as I rolled her to her belly. Her long, beautiful back stretched out in front of me, all curving lines and and soft muscle definition. I pushed aside her hair and leaned over to nibble the back of her neck. With a soft moan, her ass lifted and rubbed eagerly against my cock.

"Mm-hm, I haven't forgotten." I chuckled, leaving more biting kisses on her back. When I reached her shoulder blade, I decided that was the place. The beautiful wing-like area on her back was where I'd leave my mark on her, claim her for good.

My pulse pounded harder at the thought, cock head dripping with need. I braced one hand next to Emmaline and aimed myself at her flushed, glossy center. She pressed back just as I thrust forward, and the contact made us both moan like we couldn't help ourselves.

It was the most indescribable feeling as I pressed all the way inside. The soft grasp of her enveloping me, the hot slickness of her body, and the most delicious friction as I drew back.

I was a fucking goner. I had to make this last so she could orgasm again for my bite, but I was lost, happily drowning in sensations that made me feel so fucking good.

"Fuck, Tryn…"

I had been hypnotized by the sight of my cock disappearing into her, her ass cheeks bouncing off my lower stomach, when her voice pulled my attention to her face. Emmaline looked back at me, her expression in a grimace of ecstasy. Her chest pressed down into the picnic blanket while her ass lifted higher, wanting even more of me.

"Emmaline," I growled, my hands settling into the dips of her waist. My thrusts went harder as my fingers dug into her flesh, the impact of her skin on mine starting to echo through the valley.

"Fuck! Yes!" Her little fists curled around the blanket, anchoring herself down to take everything I gave her.

"Oh, you're close, aren't you?" I felt her squeeze around my length, noticed her breaths getting shorter and her skin flushing with heat. "So close to milking my cock 'cause I'm fucking you so good."

"Mm, yes! Don't stop, Tryn. Fuck, please don't stop…"

"Not on your life." I bowed over her again and found that perfect spot on her shoulder blade with my lips.

I kissed her there tenderly while thrusting at a constant, steady pace. She felt so good, my own control felt like a thread ready to snap. But I held on, marching her closer and closer to bliss.

She was on the edge, trembling with the need to release

when I brought the skin of her shoulder blade between my teeth. But I didn't bite down, not yet. I brought my hand underneath her and found her clit. With two swipes of my fingers and a few more thrusts, she exploded into bliss and I bit down hard.

Emmaline thrashed beneath me, and I let go of the bite as soon as I tasted blood. I wanted to lick the wound, to soothe and heal it, but she shook so hard from the orgasm that I slipped out of her.

"Emmaline." I hovered over her, not caring about my own pleasure in that moment but only the well being of my mate. She lay on her stomach, panting hard. I stroked her hair, kissed the side of her face, and licked away the blood from my bite. "Emmaline, are you okay?"

She rolled over and started to sit up, so I backed away to give her space. When I saw tears shining in her eyes, my concern hit a new high. "What's wrong?" I demanded, cupping her face. "Fuck, did I hurt you?"

"No..."

The single word was a breathy whisper, accompanied by a smile. She brought a hand to her chest, right over the fate thread that connected us. It seemed like she could feel the thread now. Even if she couldn't see it, she could feel it like it was a tangible, real thing.

"I can feel you here," she whispered in awe and laughed lightly. "You can stop worrying. I'm fine."

"Are you sure?"

"Yes. I, wow..." She looked up at me with shock and wonder in her features. "You really feel this way about me? You...love me this much?"

I touched my forehead and nose to hers. "Fuck yes."

With my bite, she had a piece of me with her. She'd be

able to sense my mood, proximity, and all my deeper feelings. It was vulnerable as hell to share that with someone, but I couldn't imagine my heart in anyone else's hands.

There would be no more secrets between us, ever.

I held my mate in my arms and kissed her while she settled and got used to the effects of my bite. After a few minutes, she lifted out of my lap and spread her legs to straddle me. With a wicked grin she said, "Your turn."

"Sweet fate, please," I moaned.

Emmaline wrapped her hand around the base of my cock and gave it a few long, firm strokes to bring me back to full hardness. Then, holding me in place, she sank down and I was fully seated in bliss again.

"You feel so fucking incredible, I can hardly breathe." I wrapped my arms around her back, holding her loosely as she lifted and lowered herself in a slow, tantalizing rhythm.

"I was scared you might be too big at first." Emmaline held onto my shoulders for leverage, her smile kissing against my mine. "But...mmm...you're making me feel good in places I didn't know existed." She started riding me harder, grasping at words as the pleasure started to overtake her.

"Fate would make sure that our bodies fit together perfectly." My fingers brushed over the bite on her shoulder blade and she shivered. "Hurt?" I asked, lifting my touch away.

"No, just tender." She kissed me deeply, her soft moans filling my mouth. "Where should I bite you?"

"Anywhere you want." I went for her nipples, teasing and sucking the little peaks since they were bouncing so prettily in my face. "My body is yours. Claim any part of it that you like."

"Hmm..." Emmaline kissed me in several places, testing out where to bite. She sucked the juncture of my neck and shoulder and seemed decided. That was until her mouth skimmed to the top of my shoulder, teeth dragging over the round muscle.

We moaned in unison, my hips snapping up as she crashed down on me. "Won't be long, beautiful." My arms locked around her waist, the urge to rut and fill up her perfect pussy taking over my senses.

"Yes, harder," she whimpered. "Fuck me, Tryn."

No male in his right mind would ever ignore a demand like that. My heels dug into the ground while I drove into her with hard, almost violent thrusts. She hung onto my shoulders, nails biting into my skin as I fucked her so hard that her ass slapped against my thighs.

I chased that perfect, elusive pleasure like a horse at a racetrack, fucking harder and getting closer, closer...

Pleasure exploded through me in a blinding surge. I felt it through the length of my cock and also, strangely, on my right shoulder. My whole body pulsed like a heartbeat, the pleasure gently ebbing with each thumping beat.

I relaxed my hold around Emmaline, only then realizing how tightly I'd clutched her. She didn't seem bothered as she gently licked and kissed my shoulder. When she lifted away with a smile, I saw it. Two crescent marks.

Something flared up in my chest, a feeling like worry or apprehension.

"Did I do it right?" Emmaline frowned, softly running her finger over the marks.

My whole body shuddered with sensitivity, like I was already on the verge of another orgasm.

"Yes," I gasped, realizing it was her insecurity that I had felt. "It's done, beautiful. You did it perfectly."

Her smile lit up her whole face, and the warmth I felt was a mix of hers and my own. Damn, now I knew why she'd been teary-eyed. It was overwhelming in the best way to feel your partner's love for you inside your own chest.

"*We* did it." She beamed so beautifully, it was a sight I'd never forget.

"We did." Wrapped up in each other, we slid to recline on the ground and just bask in this feeling.

Fate may have chosen us for each other, but *we* overcame the odds. *We* fought our way back to each other to get to this point.

And we won.

EPILOGUE
EMMALINE

Tryn was waiting for me as I came out of Derric's office. "So? How'd it go?"

I smiled at the bright eagerness in his voice. "Let's go for a walk."

He smiled back. "On four legs or two?"

"Let's do two."

He held the lodge door open for me and together, we walked out into the crisp, fresh air. I inhaled deeply, taking in the scent of pine, fresh earth, and nearby wolves all into my lungs. It was hard to believe Vargmore had been my home for a week already. I felt like I'd returned home, not just moved to a new place.

Tryn said we could start looking for our own place soon, but I actually enjoyed living at the Howling Death lodge. I liked that there were always people nearby, sharing the kitchen and communal living areas. When I wanted privacy, Tryn's bedroom was my favorite, cozy place to retreat. Everything smelled like him, and I couldn't get enough of wrapping his scent around me.

"Well?" Tryn laced his fingers through mine, walking calmly at my side, but I could sense his anticipation.

I grinned, unable to hold it in any longer. "The Alpha said yes!"

"Really? To everything?"

"Well, he laid out very strict but reasonable rules, but yes. I can go to the human world to attend conferences and get medical journals." One thing that remained important to me was keeping my veterinary skills sharp and up-to-date, and that meant leaving one foot in the human world. Thankfully, Derric heard me out and was agreeable to me making occasional trips back and forth from Vargmore.

"That's great news!" Tryn turned and embraced me hard before kissing me deeply, his warm hands holding my face. "I'm so glad you can still pursue your dreams." With a low growl he added, "I would've had words with Derric if he didn't allow it, but it seems he's softened up to humans recently."

"I think it helps that I'll be able to treat the pack. We also talked about me ordering some advanced medical equipment. An ultrasound machine, surgical tools, things like that. He's going to have Orson make a budget and get back to me."

"More great news." Tryn beamed. "The witches are skilled healers, but they don't know everything you do."

"Their tools are just different," I said. "I don't have magic and ancient knowledge of herbs at my disposal, but I hope my own skill set can be useful."

"You saved my ass, didn't you?" He nuzzled my temple and kissed me there.

"I had help," I reminded him. "And you saved me first, remember?"

"If it were your guts in danger of falling out, I'd be pretty damn useless, so I think you win the best savior award."

"Oh, shut up." I laughed, hooking my arm through his as we walked. "We can both be dashing heroes and damsels in distress."

Tryn chuckled. "Only for each other."

"Definitely."

We walked quietly for a while along a winding, gravel road. I'd walked this way enough times already to know that we'd reach Stout & Spirit eventually. Yesterday, I offered to help Shiloh behind the bar a couple days a week and she practically jumped for joy.

The future looked bright. I had my love, my passion, a real home, and others like me. But for the moment, my mind was stuck on one little detail of the past.

"Can I ask you to do me a favor?" My arm tightened around Tryn's bicep.

"Anything," he said without hesitation, and I knew that he meant it.

I took a deep breath. "I'd like to visit my parents, and I'd love it if you came with me."

Tryn paused and turned to face me. "Of course I will, beautiful." His expression implored me to explain further. After I told him more about my family situation, that they were so strict with me academically and never supported me becoming a vet, he wasn't the biggest fan of my parents.

"I'm going to reduce contact with them after this visit," I said. "But I've been avoiding them for over a month, and I think they deserve to know some version of what's going on with me. Not specifics, of course. But I want to tell them that I fell in love, I'm still practicing veterinary medicine, and I'm happy living a quiet life in the mountains."

"Do you think they'll approve? Now that you finally are happy?" Tryn asked.

I barked out a harsh laugh. "Not a chance. I'm sure they'll keep arguing that I need to go to law school or something, but I don't care. I don't need their approval anymore. That's why I'm reducing contact. I just...need to do this. I need to tell them that I'm finally taking control of my life, and I'm choosing happiness."

Tryn nodded and took my hands in his. "This is important to you, so of course I'll be there to support you." He drew me forward and kissed me before continuing. "But I'm warning you right now, if they try to disrespect you or talk down to you in any way, I'm calling it out. I don't care if they're your parents, no one gets away with putting down my mate."

Although the human side of me was just a touch worried about being caught in the middle of such a confrontation, my wolf absolutely loved hearing this from him. Our mate was protective and strong. Fate had chosen well for us. Whether such a confrontation came or not, I had to agree with her there.

"Well, hopefully they'll be on their best behavior and it won't have to come to that." I reached on tiptoes to kiss Tryn again.

"I promise you *I* will be," he murmured against my lips.

My smile touched his. "I know you will."

"Until a situation calls for me to misbehave." He grabbed my ass and kissed me deeper, right there in the middle of the road.

I was trying to decide if we should sneak off into the

trees or wait until we got back to the lodge when I heard someone crying out.

"Hey! I need some help!"

I broke away from Tryn and whipped around to see Orson running toward us. His expression was unlike any I'd seen before, a hard mix of worry and fury.

"What's wrong?" Tryn demanded.

"Is Shiloh okay?" I couldn't imagine anyone except his mate making him this frantic.

"It's not Shiloh, she's fine." Orson panted heavily. "It's Nova, my sister."

"Oh." I hadn't met his sister and didn't know that he had one, but that wasn't important right now. "Where is she? What happened?" I started speed walking alongside Orson in the direction he came from, ready to help in any way that I could. Tryn was right there with me.

"She came down from the mountain and just collapsed. I—I don't know."

"She left the feral pack?" Tryn asked.

"I don't know, she must have." Realizing he had to clue me in, Orson said, "My half-sister has lived with a feral pack of werewolves deep in the mountains. They're really roughing it out there; no modern technology, medicine, or anything. Not even electricity or plumbing."

"Okay. Did she look injured to you? Any blood or bruising on her that you could see?"

"No, I don't think so." He pointed to a figure lying on the ground a few feet ahead. "There she is. I was scared to move her, so I just ran for help."

"You did the right thing," Tryn assured him. "I'll call Derric. She'll be okay, Ors."

While Tryn calmed his frantic packmate, I knelt on the

ground and looked over my new patient. She had a fluttery pulse and was breathing shallowly, but at least she was alive. I couldn't find any broken bones or other major injuries. Her skin lacked elasticity, which meant she was dehydrated. The more I checked her over, the more confident I became that she was simply dehydrated and exhausted.

"She's going to be fine," I announced as Derric and Ruse arrived. "She just needs rest and fluids. Let's take her back to the lodge, and I can set up an IV for her."

"Oh, thank the moon." Orson sagged with relief. His icy blue eyes were, for once, filled with warmth. "Thank you, Emmaline. I'm so glad you're here."

"It's no problem." I looked at the four male werewolves standing around. "Who wants to carry her back?"

Orson and Ruse both stepped forward. When Orson let out a protective growl, Ruse shocked everyone by growling back.

"She's my blood," Orson snarled. "Back off."

"Ruse," Derric snapped. "Stand down. Let him carry her."

Only that seemed to snap the VP out of it. Ruse shook his head, brow furrowing like he was confused. "Sorry, Alpha. I don't know what got into me."

Tryn's eyes met mine as Orson scooped up his sister, and we exchanged the same high-eyebrowed look. As our group headed back to the lodge, my mate and I trailed behind.

"See anything interesting?" I asked when the others were out of earshot.

"Most definitely," he answered with a knowing smirk.

"Something like a fate thread, perhaps?"

"Something like that." He brought an arm around my shoulders, fingers stroking over his mating bite on my back. "It'll be interesting to see how that plays out."

My fingers laced with his resting on my shoulder. "I still think we're the best pair fate ever brought together."

He held my chin and turned my head to face him. "I couldn't agree more, beautiful." We kissed long and deep, just how we liked it. And then followed our packmates home.

)))))♪♪♪◖◖◖◖◖◖

Thank you so much for reading Cursed Wolf! I hope you enjoyed Tryn and Emmaline's story.

Are you dying to see Emmaline confront her parents with her sexy, growly biker backing her up?
Grab that bonus scene here:
https://BookHip.com/XHNHQDT

)))))♪♪♪◖◖◖◖◖◖

If you want more of the Howling Death werewolves, I recommend starting with Sawyer's book, Traitor Wolf. What's an enforcer to do when a human turns up on his turf smelling like enemy vampires?

Start reading Traitor Wolf:
https://books2read.com/traitorwolf

Also by Sophie Ash

<u>Gods and Myths</u>

The Minotaur

<u>Howling Death MC</u>

Traitor Wolf

Enemy Wolf

Cursed Wolf

About the Author

Sophie Ash is a USA Today bestselling author from Northern California, writing paranormal romances with plenty of bite, as well as passionate retellings of myths and folklore.

When she's not writing, she's probably reading, gardening, vacuuming up cat hair, or enjoying a craft beer in the sun.

Sign up for Sophie's email list and get a free standalone novella as a thank you gift: https://BookHip.com/KBRCFWN

facebook.com/Crystal.Sophie.Ash.Books

instagram.com/crystalsophieash

amazon.com/author/sophieash

bookbub.com/profile/sophie-ash